A Bang on the Head

By
Will Stebbings

First published in 2021

A CIP catalogue record for this book is available from the British Library.

Also by Will Stebbings

OFF THE MARK – Published by Troubador Publishing Ltd

FURTHER OFF THE MARK - Published by Troubador Publishing Ltd

COMPLETELY OFF THE MARK - Published by 3P Publishing

MARK'S OUT OF ELEVEN - Published by Troubador Publishing Ltd

TESS OF THE DORMOBILES - Published by KDP

Chapter 1

Rob Lennard was awake, but reluctant to open his eyes. He had been dreaming and wanted to return to that mysterious world where nothing made sense. An unfamiliar sound had woken him from his disturbed slumber and his head was throbbing. Through his closed eyelids, he could sense a light that wasn't normally there in his bedroom. He opened them. The light was coming through a gap in the curtains, but these were not the curtains of his bedroom. He needed his spectacles. He normally kept them close at hand beside the bed, but the bedside table was higher than usual and he couldn't reach without moving his whole body and that hurt his head to do so. He decided the pain was too much to justify the effort.

He found himself imprisoned within two guard rails. He was also aware of tubes hanging down beside the bed, but without his spectacles, he couldn't see what was happening. Nevertheless, it didn't take him long to realise that he was in a hospital bed. This was confirmed by the noise of quiet voices and shuffling feet a few yards away. He'd never been admitted to a hospital before and he wondered why he was there. Had he been involved in a road accident?

Suddenly, the curtains were thrown back and a pleasing shape appeared. 'Oh, you're awake at last,' the pleasing shape uttered.

'Where am I?' he asked.

'You're in the hospital of course,' the nurse replied. 'I'm Staff Nurse Tracy. How do you feel?'

'Like my head is going to explode. What's happened?'

'I understand you had a fight with a big tree – and the tree won by all accounts. Don't you remember?'

'No, I don't remember anything,' he said, scrunching his face through the pain. 'Can I have my glasses?' He hated trying to talk to someone without his spectacles and he wanted to see who owned that comforting voice.
'They're probably in your cupboard. Your wife will be pleased that you've come around at last. You've been out for two days. Now, let's have a look in here.'
'I haven't got a wife,' he replied.
'Oh ... my mistake. Is she your partner?'
'I haven't got a partner,' he was puzzled. To him, a partner meant business partner and he wasn't in business.
'She said her name was Mrs. Lennard,' Tracy said, also feeling puzzled.
'That must be my mother, then,' he said.
'I don't think so. She looked a little younger than you ... in her fifties I would think at a guess. Here they are.'
'How old do you think I am?' he exclaimed with some disgust. 'And these are not my glasses.'
'I know how old you are. I've seen your notes. You're sixty years old ... and those are your spectacles. I have a feeling that you've got a touch of amnesia! Are you in any pain?'
'Sixty?' He couldn't believe his ears. 'Are you telling me that I've been asleep for forty years?'
'Don't be silly. You've been unconscious for just over two days. Are you telling me that you think you're just twenty years old?'
'I am twenty. Look at me. Do I look sixty to you?'
'Yes. I'm going to get the doctor to examine you again. You had a nasty blow to the head. Are you in pain?' she patiently repeated the question.
His head was swimming around. Was he still dreaming? He went to pinch himself but saw the cannula in the back of his hand with the tube leading to a drip on a stand. Surprisingly, he could see clearly with

these unfamiliar glasses. 'Yes, I'm in a lot of pain,' he replied.
'On a scale of one to ten, how bad is it,' she asked.
'I don't know. It's bad,' he replied.
'I need to know how bad. If a toothache is a score of nine, how high is your pain and where is it?'
'I suppose it's about seven or eight,' he replied. 'And it's all over my whole skull.'
'I'll get you some painkillers,' she said. 'Meanwhile, I think you need to rest.'
'I don't need to rest. You told me that I've been asleep for two days!'
'You still need to recover. Just lay back while I fetch your medication.'
He flopped his head back on the pillow and immediately regretted his action. It hurt. He used his left hand to feel the wound and found his head was completely bandaged. He closed his eyes and tried to make sense of it all. The last thing he remembered was Sunday morning's game of football against the Bell Inn and returning home to prepare for a meeting with his girlfriend, Kate. It certainly sounded like he had suffered a very severe case of amnesia. If he was sixty, this must be the year 2019. What had happened during those missing forty years?
This Mrs Lennard that the nurse had mentioned, could that be Kate? Had he married his sweetheart and forgotten all about it? If this really was 2019, there must surely have been tremendous changes since the days of his memories of 1979. Did everyone now move around by jetpacks or spaceships? Do men live on Mars?
As he was contemplating all these things, Nurse Tracy returned with a cabinet on wheels.
'Here you are,' she said. 'I've brought all your medication as well as some paracetamol. I've spoken

to your wife and told her about your amnesia. She said she is going to call you on your mobile. Perhaps if you hear her voice, it might trigger off your memory.'
'What's a mobile?' he asked.
'Your mobile 'phone of course. She said she put it in your cupboard ready for when you wake up. If the paracetamol doesn't do the trick, I'll ask the doctor if we can set up a morphine drip, but it tends to make you drowsy so we'll start with the pills. Now, I see you're on ramipril and statins. I don't suppose you know what time of day you normally have these do you?'
'Why do I need rami ... pril and statins?' he asked.
'The ramipril is for your blood pressure and the statins are to keep your cholesterol under control. This is normal for someone your age, but your dosage of each seems quite low and we've been checking your blood pressure regularly. It's a little on the low side. That's not too unusual given the circumstances. I think we'll leave the regular medication for now. Just sit up a little, will you?'
She passed him a glass of water and he took the pain killers.'
Just then, there was a musical sound from the cupboard beside his bed. 'That'll be her, I expect' and she rummaged in the cupboard to produce his 'phone.
It looked liked nothing he had ever seen before. It certainly didn't resemble a 'phone.
Tracy answered the call. 'Yes, he's right here. I'll pass you onto him.'
He looked at it with suspicion, but decided that it must be a modern version of a walkie-talkie, although he could see neither mouthpiece nor ear-piece, but he'd seen the nurse hold it to her ear.
'Wrong way up,' she said as he held it tentatively with his left hand, the other being connected to a drip.

'Hello,' he said and then took it away from his face and looked at it again. There were pictures on a screen.
He heard a voice coming from this strange contraption.
'Rob?' the voice said. 'Are you there?'
'Talk to her,' Nurse Tracy said.
'Hello ... over,' he said. He thought when people used walkie-talkies, they had to say 'over' to let the other party know they had finished talking. He held the 'phone to his head but still didn't know where the earpiece was.
'Rob, thank Heaven you've come around at last,' the voice said. 'We've been so worried about you.'
'Is that Kate?' he asked, forgetting to say 'over.'
'Kate? What are you on about? It's Julie ... your wife, silly. Who's this Kate? Look, I know the nurse said you've probably got a bit of concussion or something. I'm coming over as soon as I've let the children know that you've woken up. They've all been so concerned. You know you scared young Barney when you hit that tree. He'll probably be scarred for life, poor little chap. I'll say goodbye for now. I'll see you soon. 'Bye.'
Rob didn't speak immediately, and then he said 'Goodbye ... over and out.' He handed the 'phone back to the nurse. 'That's a remarkable piece of equipment,' he said as he did so. 'How much would something like that cost?'
'I think most people have them on contract. I have an older model and I pay about thirty pounds a month. Some people pay more; some people pay less. It depends on the network and other things like the amount of call time, the memory and download options.'
'I don't understand any of that,' he said.
'I haven't really got time to explain at the moment,' Tracy said. 'When your wife comes, perhaps she can explain it. For now, lie back and let the painkillers do

their job. I'll be back later. We'll probably need to change your sheets and give you a wash. Drink plenty of water. It's important to keep your fluids up.'
'I think I need to use the toilet,' he said, feeling a little embarrassed.
'Do you mean you want to empty your bowels? 'Cause you've got a catheter for your bladder. Just do it if you haven't already.' That was when he noticed a tube leading out from under the blanket.
'Oh,' he said. '... that's all right, then.'
He waited until she left before he pulled back the blanket to see his member with a tube held in place by a dressing. Someone must have handled his member to insert that. He was glad he wasn't awake for that, but he felt helpless. What else had they done to him while he was unconscious? He lay back and tried not to think about it. He had other things on his mind.
What sort of world was this year 2019? Was it the space age that had been predicted back in the seventies? With a little imagination, that mobile 'phone could be one of the communicators that they used in *Star Trek*. Perhaps they now had some other means of propulsion – an equivalent to dilithium crystals. Surely after forty years, the world's petrol resources would have been exhausted, meaning a much cleaner environment. They'd probably finally tackled the problem of nuclear fusion, providing cheap electricity; if not, hydro electricity perhaps? There would be huge dams across the Lake District. Newlands Valley would have been flooded, swallowing up little hamlets like Little Town.
And what about all these robots that were going to do a lot of the work so that everyone had more leisure time and men could work a four day week, then retire at fifty five? Women would not have to work at all, except for those roles traditionally carried out by females, such as

nursing and secretarial work; a truly brave new world ... or probably not. Who knows? He would find out soon. If only he could look out of the window, but he was in an isolation bed surrounded by curtains.
He realised that the pain had lessened. The tablets must have worked, but he still felt most uncomfortable and there was nothing to take his mind off his situation. He was looking forward to the return of the charming Nurse Tracy – or even a visit from the doctor. He needed more answers.

Chapter 2

Julie was anxious to get to the hospital to see her husband. His accident with the tree had upset everyone. Somehow, no one in the family expected Rob to ever have to visit a hospital. But before she could make her way there, she had to 'phone their daughter, Sarah, to tell her the news that Rob was awake and ask her to tell Barney who had been particularly upset. He loved his grandad. Julie also asked Sarah to inform her brother Ben so as to save her time. Ben and his family still lived in Norfolk and hadn't been present at the time of the accident but had been equally as upset over the bad news.

Julie's next action was to send an e-mail to her two team leaders at work. After the accident, she had arranged to work from home so that she could quickly react if anything happened and this e-mail to them both warned that she would be away from her computer for an hour or two. She always believed that a good manager could organise herself so that any absence was not felt by the business and she trusted her two colleagues to cope in her absence.

They were two completely different characters. Jerry was inclined to take on all the work himself instead of delegating to his less experienced team members. This meant that when Julie conducted her monthly meetings with her two leaders, Jerry was seldom able to announce completion of his action points and always had an excuse for not doing so. In direct contrast, Bernie made a point of ensuring that all his action points were completed or at least had been progressed and he believed his team responded better if trusted with the work. Julie also knew that Bernie was in awe of her. Her stature helped in this respect because she

stood at least four inches taller than him and she had often seen him gazing at her bosom and her shapely legs. She had never seen Jerry staring at her bosom. Perhaps that was because he was a similar height to her.
She was soon on her way to the hospital which was a good thirty minutes drive away. As she drove, she thought about what the nurse had said about Rob suffering from amnesia. How much did he remember? And who was Kate? She might be one of his clients, since he didn't talk much about them, feeling a personal trainer owed his clients a certain level of confidentiality. She was sure that as soon as she started talking about little Barney and the family, he would start to remember things. He loved them all and they loved him.

As the pain eased a little more, Rob became more aware of his surroundings. He now realised that he had wires attached between him and some kind of monitoring equipment.
He still couldn't remember anything beyond that weekend in 1979. He just wanted to see Kate. It seemed highly unlikely that she was aware of his predicament. He had been looking forward to their next meeting when he was going to brooch the subject of marriage. They had both already expressed their love for one another and he wanted to take their relationship to the next stage. Their finances did not reach to actually getting married at that time, but he wanted a commitment ... except that that was forty years ago. What had happened to her? Had they married and then split up? Had she rejected him? Surely not. She had already told him how much she loved him.
As he was pondering all this, Nurse Tracy reappeared with a male doctor who was studying a file. Neither

spoke for a minute, then the doctor said 'Right, Mr Lennard. I'm Doctor Shah, the duty doctor. I understand you're struggling to remember recent events. Tell me what you do remember.'

The sixty year-old Rob was a self-confident individual who could have easily conveyed his thoughts to a stranger, but the twenty year old version was a little shy, especially in the presence of an attractive young lady and another figure of some authority. He hesitated before replying.

'Well ... if you mean 1979, I can clearly remember lots of things ... everything really, but ... I don't know anything about ... 2019.' The year sounded strange in his mind. It seemed like a year from a science fiction film.

'So you don't recall anything about your little accident?'

'I don't know anything about an accident. What happened?'

The doctor looked as though he didn't have time for any kind of conversation so Tracy responded. 'I'm told that you were playing football in your garden and you slipped and hit your head on a tree. Then to make things worse, as you fell back, you cracked your head against a stone in your rockery. We think the first blow knocked you unconscious and it was the second that caused the bleeding. You had to have stitches in the head wound. At the moment, you have a dressing over it to protect it from infection.'

'How is the pain, now?' the doctor asked.

'It's a lot better than it was, but I still feel it when I move my head.' To prove it, he moved his head and winced.

The doctor had another look at the file and said 'It's not unusual for concussion to cause loss of memory, but it's usually a matter of being unable to remember things in your short memory. I've never heard of anyone losing forty years worth of memory like this, especially as you seem to have very clear recollection of 1979, but this is not my specialist field. We're going to keep you in for a few days and monitor your progress and see if we can get your memory restored. We'll get one of my colleagues to attend you as soon as we can. Meanwhile, we need this bed for another patient so we'll move you down to the ward. Can you arrange that, Nurse? We can probably lose the drip and the catheter.'

With that, he handed the file to the nurse and left. Rob felt as though he was an inconvenience, but Nurse Tracy was much more caring. 'I'll just take your blood pressure and temperature before we think about moving you,' she said with a reassuring smile that made him feel better, but it occurred to him that she would be the one removing the catheter. When he had looked at it, he had been surprised that his member had shrunk alarmingly. Is this what happens when you reach sixty? This was going to be embarrassing. There was no doubt that she would have seen all different sizes while performing her job, but his had shrunk to almost nothing.

She disappeared for a few minutes then came back with her equipment. 'I'll just take some blood for testing. We need to make sure you haven't got any infection. Now are you ready? Now ... it's just a little prick.'

He immediately thought of one of the hospital-based *Carry On* films where a similar remark had been made for comic effect. He hoped Nurse Tracy was not trying to be amusing. He looked to see her extracting a small amount of blood. 'Just put your hand on that,' she said as she placed a piece of cotton wool over the small wound in his arm. 'I'll move around to your other arm to take your blood pressure.'

She did so and secured the strapping around his arm. This was the very first time that he could remember

having his blood pressure taken, although, of course, the procedure must have been performed numerous times if he was already on medication. 'Give me your finger,' she said and clipped something to the end of it. He had no idea what that was. As she pressed a button on the sphygmomanometer, she said 'We'll just take your temperature.' He opened his mouth to receive a thermometer; instead, she said 'No, I want your ear.' The device was in and out in two seconds. 'That's all right,' she said.
He was amazed at this device. It put him in mind of the devices Doctor McCoy used in *Star Trek*.
Just then, the pressure on his arm increased alarmingly. The machine seemed to stop and then start up again, piling on even more pressure. He thought something had gone wrong and felt like telling her. The pressure was becoming unbearable, but then it suddenly released and she looked at the display. 'Mmm ... still just a little low ... but nothing to worry about. When you're unconscious, the body kind of slows down some of its functions. You'll soon be back to normal, but we'll keeping watching it. I'll advise your new nursing staff to lay off the Ramipril for a while.'
She then proceeded to disconnect the drip. 'We'll leave the cannula in case we need to give you some anti-biotic.' She moved the stand for the drip and said 'Right, let's get rid of this catheter. It will be a little uncomfortable, but the sooner we do it, the better. I'll just get you a pad so you can prevent any leakage.'
She pulled back the sheets and lifted his gown to expose his appendage – or what was left of it.'
'Will it get back to normal size?' he asked, thinking he needed to explain its small size.
'Oh, yes,' she said with a smile. 'It's normal after what you've been through for it to shrink. Now hold that pad

ready. Here we go.' She was used to men feeling self-conscious about their size.
She pulled the catheter out in a smooth operation as he gritted his teeth. It was an unpleasant sensation, but Tracy was expert and moved away with the tube and bag to dispose of the contents while Rob covered his dignity with the pad.

Forty minutes later, Rob was in a different bed in a different ward receiving the attention of two different nurses. They had introduced themselves, but their names didn't register as they rushed in to ask questions about his condition. He was disappointed that Nurse Tracy hadn't followed him downstairs. He had taken quite a shine to her and although these new nurses were nice enough, they weren't Nurse Tracy. He also noticed that each wore a different coloured uniform. He wondered if this represented their rank or perhaps their function like the uniforms on *Star Trek.* Would they have a Chief Science Officer? One wore a light blue uniform, the other a darker blue. Tracy had worn white.
After pummelling him with questions about what he could remember, the one of obvious Asian origin said 'It's a bit like *Back to the Future*, isn't it?'
Rob didn't understand the significance of this as the film hadn't been released until 1985.
Just then a tea trolley arrived and he was asked if he wanted a cup of tea or coffee. 'Have you eaten at all?' the white nurse asked.
'Not since 1979,' he answered.
'You must be very hungry,' the Asian nurse said with a laugh that bordered on a giggle. 'I'll see if I can find a biscuit for you. You will have to content yourself with a sandwich at lunchtime but perhaps something more substantial for tea. We'll see what the doctors say.'

They then demonstrated how to use the control to raise his bed to allow him to sit up to drink his tea. They also pointed out the button for summoning help if he needed it and advised that the doctors would be doing the rounds soon. 'We'll have to get you moving around in a little while,' one of them said. 'You don't want to get any bed sores.'

Rob was enjoying his tea and digestive biscuits when he heard voices down the corridor.

'Visiting hours are two to four,' he heard.

'I was told to come and talk to him to help his memory,' another voice said.

'Oh, yes ... you'll find him in the end bed behind the curtains.' The use of the word *memory* meant that they were surely talking about him.

The curtains were flung back and there stood an imposing female figure. Rob guessed that the nurses would have had difficulty in stopping her visiting.

'There you are. I've been all over the hospital trying to find you. No one told me that you'd been moved. Now what's all this nonsense about losing your memory?'

Was this the woman with whom he had spent the last so many years? She was the exact opposite of his Kate. Julie was almost six feet tall and built like the lady in the Commodores' song – a brick-house. He imagined her 'letting it all hang out.' Kate was petite with small but well-formed breasts. Julie's breasts had entered through the curtains a good half-second before the rest of her. And where Kate was quiet and shy, Julie ... wasn't!

'Are you my wife?' he asked gingerly.

She let out a sigh. 'Is this some kind of a joke? We've only been married for thirty five years. This is a lot of nonsense.'

'I'm sorry,' he said, 'but I don't remember anything after 1979.'

She let out another sigh. 'Why 1979? I didn't even know you then? How can I help your memory if I've nowhere to start from? Let's try Sunday afternoon. Sarah and Neville had brought little Barney round for lunch – Sarah is our daughter ... married to Neville and Barney is their son ... five years old. Okay?'
Rob nodded and said 'I've got a grandson?'
'You've got two actually. The other one is Ben's son ... Ben is your son and Sarah also has a daughter, so you have three grandchildren. Anyway, Barney loves to play football with you in the back garden. You told him you were getting too old and he should play with his dad. Barney said "*Dad's rubbish. You play, Grandad.*" So the three of you played and you were showing off with your dribbles and ball control when you slipped on a tree root. You hit the tree and fell back banging your head on the rockery. Does any of this ring a bell?'
'No, he said, 'other than Tracy already told me that I banged my head twice.'
'Who's Tracy?' she demanded.
'The nurse upstairs.'
'Oh, right ... anyway, Barney said "*Mum, Grandad's fallen asleep. Wake up, Grandad!*" Then he saw the blood pouring out of your head and said *"Nanny, Grandad needs a plaster."*
'He sounds like a lovely little lad. I shall look forward to meeting him.'
'What do you mean *meeting him*? You've already met him. He's your grandson! Wait a minute; I've got a 'photo of him here.' She went to her handbag and pulled out her mobile 'phone. After a few minutes scrolling and swiping, she handed it him.
He took it and stared. 'How do you get a photograph onto this device? It's amazing.'
'You've got the same 'photo on your 'phone,' she said. 'I sent it to you.'

'You can send photographs to a 'phone?'
'Of course you can. Where's your 'phone? I'll show you.' She looked in his cupboard and found it. 'Damn, the battery is low.'
'Have you got a spare battery?' he asked.
'You don't replace the battery. You recharge it. I'll bring your charger in next time I come.'
Rob thought of the battery charger he once borrowed from a neighbour to recharge his car battery. They must have made them smaller by now. He took another look at the 'photo on the 'phone still in his hand. 'He looks like a smashing lad. Do they live nearby?' he asked.
'They live in Ketton.'
Rob had never heard of Ketton and said so. 'Is it still in Norfolk?'
'Of course not. We left Norfolk ten years ago. Ben still lives there. They have a house in North Wootton.'
'So where do we live?' Rob asked.
'South Luffenham,' she replied.
'Where's that?' he asked.
'Near Ketton,' she said, then seeing the look of annoyance on his face, added 'It's in Rutland – halfway between Stamford and Uppingham.'
'So this isn't King's Lynn hospital?' he asked.
'No, it's Peterborough. It's a nice hospital – apart from the parking. You struggle to find a parking space and then you have to pay a fortune to get out.'
Rob wasn't really interested in parking problems. He still had one burning question. He knew it wouldn't go down well, but he had to know. 'Do you know what happened to Kate?'
'Kate who?'
'Kate Sanderson. The girl I was going to marry.'
'Oh, her! She died in a car accident. That was well before you met me.'

Rob felt like he'd been thumped in the chest. 'Kate's ... dead? No, she can't be.' He tried to suppress his tears, but he could feel them flowing from the edge of his eyes. He turned his head away from his wife.
'This is silly,' she said. 'That was nearly forty years ago. You got over all that ages ago.'
But Rob was inconsolable. He couldn't look at his wife.
Just then the doctor arrived doing his morning rounds. He was accompanied by one of the nurses and two other people, both looking absurdly young. One of those, a young dark skinned girl was holding a laptop propped open and resting on one arm.
The doctor didn't speak, but picked up Rob's notes and studied them for a minute, then looked up at Rob and his wife. 'So this is Robert Lennard ... and Mrs Lennard?' He didn't wait for a reply. 'Concussion and lesions to the skull ... only recently woken from a two day coma and suffering loss of memory. How are you feeling, Mr. Lennard?'
Rob was still trying to recover his composure and took a few seconds before replying. 'I'm getting better,' but then he remembered the news about Kate and closed his eyes before trying to speak again.
The doctor saw the tears still trickling down his cheeks. 'What's this? Are you in a lot of pain?'
Julie intervened 'He's just heard that his old girlfriend died forty years ago.'
'And he's only just heard the news?'
'No, he heard the news all those years ago, but for some reason, he can't remember.
The nurse who had previously talked to Rob explained more about his inability to remember anything during the last forty years.
The doctor listened intently and then said 'It's not unusual for a patient to lose partial memory after a blow to the head, but this is most unusual. In fact, I suspect

the memory loss may be due to some other trauma. Do you know where you live?'
'South Luffenham ... my wife just told me.'
'Well, you seem to be all right with your short term memory.'
'And I've got two children Ben and Sarah; three grandchildren, one of whom, Barney was with me when I had my accident. That's all things I've been told this morning. Apart from that, I know nothing since 1979 ... which I remember very well.' Then he thought once more about Kate and his stomach cramped up with grief – and it showed on his face.
Julie took his hand. 'Come on, love! It was years ago.'
The doctor was more sympathetic. 'If he believes he has just heard the bad news for the first time, he will relive the grief all over again. It's like *Groundhog Day* to him.' Except that Rob had no idea what *Groundhog Day* was.
'Can't you do something for him?' Julie asked. 'People do recover from things like this don't they?'
'Usually,' said the doctor, 'but it takes time and patience. We might need to get him some kind of physiotherapy. It's not like that Laurel and Hardy film where one of them keeps receiving a knock on the head and his memory is switched off and on several times. If your husband has another knock to the head, it will probably cause a lot of harm. Now, if you don't mind, I think you should come back later and leave us to do a few more tests.'

Chapter 3

Julie was furious with herself. She had blundered in with all the subtlety of an articulated lorry, but how was she to know that Rob would relive the grief of losing a former sweetheart from so long ago? The whole thing didn't make sense. She had tried to talk about his real life in the hope that it would awaken his memories of recent years, but she had failed miserably. She decided to skip the afternoon visiting hours and return after six o'clock. Perhaps by then, there might be an improvement in his condition. She had to persevere by talking about his present life and recent events.

Rob was in turmoil. Had Kate suffered? What about her parents? They would have been distraught. He wanted to go and see them, but, of course, that was pointless. They would have moved on from their grief years ago. He would still like to see them.

And then there was his wife. How did that happen? She just was not his type. He liked quiet petite young girls, not this strapping woman with big breasts and a domineering voice. Perhaps he had got her in the family way after a one-night stand. Maybe she had lots of money at a time when he was desperate for funds. He needed to find out more, but he had to be tactful about his enquiries. He couldn't just ask 'How the Hell did I come to marry you?'

And then he thought again about poor sweet Kate and his insides cramped up. He wanted to be left alone, but the nurses kept coming to take his blood pressure and temperature and pointlessly asking if he had regained his memory yet.

Despite preferring his own company, when the afternoon visiting commenced, he found himself disappointed that no one came to see him. Even the nurses stayed away for nearly three hours. All the other patients in the ward had guests, but not him. By now, he was able to visit the toilet on his own. Two nice female physiotherapists had visited him earlier and insisted that he must get out of bed occasionally and have a walk around. He had felt quite shaky at first, but he soon improved. After walking him around for a while, they then declared that he was discharged from their care, but that didn't mean he could leave the hospital just yet. He would be kept in for further observation.
To make matters worse, the man in the bed opposite had three separate sets of visitors; and, in between, he seemed to spend all his time on his mobile 'phone, telling everyone about his recent surgical procedure. These new fangled devices might be brilliant for keeping in touch, but they could be so annoying for anyone close by.
Rob was relieved when the visitors finally left. There was an upright chair next to his bed, but because he had nothing to read, he felt awkward just sat there, so he soon returned to his bed. He decided that the next time he saw a nurse, he would ask if there was any reading matter around ... but the nurses stayed away for some reason and the next visitor to the ward was the lady delivering his evening meal, which turned out to be surprisingly tasty. He had selected leek and potato soup with a roll, followed by apple pie and custard, washed down with a cup of tea. At least that gave him something to do for a few minutes, but he was soon back in his bed, feeling a strange mixture of grief and boredom.
Just before the next visitors' session, a nurse appeared to take his blood pressure again. He asked her about

something to read and she said 'I'll see what I can find,' but he didn't see her again that evening.

As the evening visitors started to arrive, Rob resigned himself to two hours of listening to other patients' unwanted conversations. He had been hoping that Julie or some other member of his family would appear to offer some respite, but after what seemed an eternity, no one showed. In fact it was less than half an hour before Julie did open his curtain. Somehow, she didn't appear to be quite so daunting and he was all ready to apologise for his earlier behaviour, but before he could do that, she asked 'How are you, love? I'm sorry I'm a bit late. I wanted to call in at the petrol station to pick up a *Telegraph.* I know you like to do the cryptic crossword and the Sudoku. I've also brought today's *Express.* You probably need to catch up with events, although, for Heaven's sakes don't read all the fuss about Brexit. You know it always upsets you.'
He hadn't a clue what she was talking about. He never did the cryptic crosswords – and what on Earth were Brexit and a Sudoku?
She continued before he could say anything. 'Oh, and I brought your charger for your 'phone. Let's find somewhere to plug it in. Do you need these curtains drawn?' Before he could answer, she had pulled them back. 'Oh, you've got a television.'
Rob had spotted the appliance earlier, but assumed it was some kind of monitoring device. It didn't look like a television. Where was the tube?
Julie found a remote control and started it up. 'There doesn't appear to be any sound,' she said, pressing some buttons. Rob was amazed at the clarity of the picture. 'Let me ask someone,' she said and walked over to the man with lots of regular visitors who at that

time was momentarily between guests. ‘Do you know how to get sound?’ she asked.
‘I think you need earphones,’ the man replied whilst still fingering his mobile ‘phone.
‘I didn’t think to bring any,’ she said to Rob returning to his bedside. ‘I expect that they don’t want televisions to disturb the other patients. Never mind; I’ve brought your Kindle so you can catch up with some reading. I made sure it was charged before I left the house. Anyway, how is the head?’
At last Rob had a chance to speak. ‘It’s getting better,’ he said. ‘Look, I’m sorry about ... erm ... losing my composure earlier. The news about Kate came as a bit of a shock. I don’t normally cry. I was prepared to accept that she and I had split up for some reason, but when you said she had ...’ He didn’t want to use the last word, but Julie spotted this.
‘No, it’s me that should apologise,’ she said, ‘but how was I to know that you still loved her after all these years? You’ve hardly mentioned her in all the time I’ve known you.’
‘But that’s it,’ he said. ‘I don’t know you ... I mean, obviously, I should do, but I feel I’ve only just met you today for the first time.’
‘Well, I’m sure the doctors will make you better. Have they said any more about your condition?’
‘Not really,’ he said. ‘They are going to book me in for a scan or something, but no one has said anything since they came round this morning. The nurses don’t know anything.’
Julie spotted Rob’s chair and walked round his bed and pulled it out so that she could sit facing him. As she walked round, he appraised her figure. He decided that for a well built elderly woman she looked quite well preserved. He could understand that a sixty year old man might find her attractive, but in his mind, he was a

mere twenty years old. She walked with a light step and held herself upright, making no attempt to hide her impressive bosom.
'Can I ask you a stupid question?' he said. She smiled and nodded. 'Are we ... you and I, that is ... happily married?'
'Oh, love; Of course we are. We've had a great life together. We raised two wonderful children and now have three lovely grandchildren – and we've got a lovely home. Of course, we're happily married. I'm sure you'll soon remember.'
Although that was reassuring, he still couldn't understand why he would have married her in the first place, so he asked 'How did we meet?'
Julie welcomed the question because reliving the past might help his condition, but she also knew that in their early days he hadn't considered her to be 'his type.'
'We first met at that nightclub in Broad Street. I can never remember its name, which kept changing anyway. I went with two other girls and you went with two of your friends. One of your friends chatted up one of mine – Jessica, probably. She was always the one to attract the boys. So the three of us sat together with the three of you. Nothing happened that night, but a few days later, we all met at the same place and we all sort of paired up. My two friends ended up dancing with your two mates, but you and I sat at the table minding the drinks and the handbags. You hardly spoke to me, but we all squeezed into your friend's car for a lift home. We were both in the back pressed closely together. You eventually spoke to me and we both said we wanted to see *Raiders of the Lost Ark* at the Majestic, so a couple of nights later, we went together; just the two of us. I think you asked me almost out of politeness. I thought we had a nice time, but you didn't make any effort to ask me for another date. Jessica

started dating your friend. I think you actually preferred her to me; something that was later proven right. Jessica and your friend stopped going out together. She told me that she found him boring. She was a very attractive little thing – blonde and petite and quite quiet – the opposite of me.

'The next thing, I knew is that you started dating Jessica, but that didn't last very long and when you bumped into me in town one day, you asked me out again. After a couple of dates, I found out that you didn't enjoy her company but you had enjoyed mine on that first date.

'And that's it. We've been together ever since. Jessica was more your type in those days, but you soon saw the error of your ways.'

'That's a nice little story,' Rob said and it seemed to answer his concern about marrying such a lady.

'Has it stirred any memories?' she asked.

'Only that I remember the nightclub and the Majestic,' he said, 'but not on those occasions.'

Just then, Julie's mobile rang. She had left her handbag on Rob's bed and she rifled through it to find the device. 'It's Ben,' she said looking at it.

Rob wondered how she knew who was calling just by looking at it.

'Hello, darling. Yes, I'm with him at the moment. His head's all bandaged up and he is recovering, but I'm assuming that Sarah told you about his memory loss. Yes, well he can't remember anything since 1979. I know! I've never heard of such a thing. I've been trying to jog his memory, but I'm not getting anywhere. He doesn't even know me. Perhaps if he speaks to you, you might have more luck than me. I'll pass you over' and she handed the 'phone to Rob who looked at it with caution. This 'phone looked a little different to the one he had seen in the morning and as she handed it over,

he could see a miniature film of a bearded man about thirty years old; except that it wasn't a film.
'Hello dad,' the man in the 'phone said. 'Can you hear me?' Rob was still holding the device at arm's length.
'Is that my son?' he asked of Julie.
'Of course, it is. That's Ben. Say *hello*. He won't bite.'
'Hello Ben.'
'Cor, you look a mess,' the bearded man said. 'You need to be more careful at your age. Leave the football to someone younger.'
Rob felt like Captain Kirk talking to a screen on *The Enterprise.* In any case, in his mind, it was only a few days ago that he was playing proper football against the Bell Inn and had set up two goals for his team.
'Ben, can you hear me?' his mother called.
'Just about, mother,' Ben replied.
'Can you think of some amusing little memory that might mean something to your father? We've got to awaken something in him.'
'Let me see,' he said. He took a minute before answering. 'There was that time in the swimming pool ... when you were trying to show off to us kids. It was at the Lynn pool and you were demonstrating your racing dive ... which was great ... except that your trunks came off and floated away.'
'I remember,' Julie said. 'I'd been pestering you to buy some new trunks, but you insisted that those would last a bit longer. You did buy some the following week. I think Ben fetched the trunks but refused to let you have them back until you said "*Please Ben, can I have my trunks back.*" Does that ring a bell, Rob?'
'No ... and if it did, I would probably choose to forget it anyway. I do remember the pool at Lynn. It hadn't been open very long ... in my memory, that is.'

Julie sighed and took back the 'phone. 'Well we tried. Thank you, Ben. Give my love to the family. I'll let you know if there is any improvement.'
Rob was amazed that he could see and hear his son on that device. 'That's an amazing piece of equipment. Does he have a video camera in the room filming him?'
'No, he has a camera built into his 'phone ... like this one.' She showed him the small camera.
'That's a camera?' he said. 'Where does the film go?'
'There is no film. It's all done digitally. There's another camera on the back, see. I'll take a 'photo of you. Keep still.'
She showed him the result.
'Is that me?' he asked. 'I look dreadful ... so old.'
'You don't do too bad for your age,' Julie replied.
'Can my 'phone show the caller's face like that?' he asked.
'No, you've still got an old *pay-as-you-go* 'phone. You're too mean to get a new one. But you can take photographs with it. I'll give you a demonstration tomorrow when it's charged up.'
Julie sighed again and looked at him. 'What else can we try?' she said.
'Am I still a surveyor?' Rob asked.
'No, you packed that up a while ago. You were made redundant from your job in Lynn. You were out of work for some time and couldn't get another job as a surveyor, so, in desperation, you took a job at a call centre in Peterborough. The pay wasn't very good and you had that horrible journey every day, but we needed the money. We were in danger of defaulting on the mortgage. I had a reasonable job, but we still needed a little more money to make ends meet. I was proud of you for sticking at it.
'Then I found a good job in Peterborough, so we moved. We didn't want to live in Peterborough itself, so

after looking around for a few months, we found this lovely little cottage in South Luffenham, where we've been ever since.
'After getting too old to play football, you started going to the gym regularly. You enjoyed it so much, that you started a course and obtained a qualification. You took a part time job at another gym and eventually became a personal trainer, which you now do full time.'
'Does that mean I'm a teacher?' he said. He'd never heard the term *personal trainer.*
'In a way,' she said.
'At a school?' he asked.
'No ... mostly at a gym, but you do sometimes go round your clients' houses if they have the right facilities – many of them are women. Before you get too excited, the youngest is in her late forties.'
Rob tried not to show any enthusiasm for that news.
'Of course,' added Julie with a smile, 'you won't be able to carry on with that unless you regain your memory – unless you go on a refresher course!'
Just then, they noticed some of the visitors saying goodbyes to the other patients.
'Gosh, it looks like it's time for me to leave. I'll just put your 'phone on charge. Tomorrow – assuming that you're still here - we'll carry on trying to revive memories. I'm not giving up on you.'
She kissed him on the cheek which felt nice. He was disappointed to see her leave, despite his earlier misgivings. He thought there was a chance that he could come to love this woman, as unlikely as that had seemed earlier in the day. It would be like dating a new girlfriend, without the angst of wondering if he was making a good impression or not. It seems that he didn't need to make a favourable impression. He'd already done that thirty five years earlier.

But he still had lots of questions that needed answering. What about his family? His parents; his brother; his aunts and uncles; all his old friends and work colleagues. His parents would now be about ninety. There was every chance that they were no longer around – or worse, in his view, in an old peoples' home wasting away. He'd visited a great aunt in one once. It was a horrible experience – and he was now sixty years old himself. Would he end up in one?
The last visitor was leaving and Rob couldn't help noticing that the poor unfortunate young girl had worn enormous tears in the knees of her jeans. So this modern era hadn't managed to eradicate poverty.

Chapter 4

Once the last straggler had left, Rob got up to visit the toilet. He had been reluctant to go while visitors were around. The bed gown he wore was tied up at the back and he knew that his bare buttocks might be exposed to all and sundry. He had been unfortunate enough to witness other patients airing their views and it wasn't a pretty sight. It was one thing for other patients to have to see each others' rear quarters, but at least visitors should be spared.
As he returned, he heard the welcoming sound of the drinks trolley coming from a nearby ward. Talking to Julie had made him thirsty. He had a jug of water at his bedside but he was fed up with drinking that.
While he waited, he picked up one of the newspapers that his wife had brought for him. He needed to take his mind off his thoughts about poor Kate and he was extremely curious to see what was happening in this brave new world into which he had suddenly been thrust. Most of it made little sense, but he could see that the UK now had another female prime minister. Margaret Thatcher had only been in power a short time in his memory and hadn't yet done enough to convince him. This second woman seemed to be attracting a lot of anger as far as he could tell. What exactly was the EU and what was Brexit? He remembered Julie mentioning that it always upset him, but he was none the wiser. Like most twenty year olds, he had shown very little interest in politics, although he had cast a vote for Thatcher's party because he was sick of all the industrial action that was bringing the country down at that time. The miners in particular had flexed their might on more than one occasion and the car workers never seemed to actually do any work.

The tea lady seemed to be taking an age. He hoped he wouldn't get missed.
There was a sudden wave of activity. Two new nurses sped into view. One of them was male and seemed to be the more senior. 'Evening everyone,' he said and marched towards a wipe board where he proceeded to write two names – *Derek* and *Jasmine*.
Derek spotted Rob and swept towards him. 'A new patient,' he said, picking up Rob's notes. 'Ah, yes, I've heard about you, Mr Lennard ... loss of memory and concussion. Do you like to be called Robert? Or Bob, perhaps?'
Rob almost replied 'Lennie,' because most of his footballing pals called him that as a contraction of his surname, but replied 'I think most people call me Rob.'
'Well, Rob, I'm Derek. Jasmine and I will be attending to you tonight. How is the head?'
'It's still a bit sore,' Rob replied, 'but I think the pain is getting less.'
'Good. We'll get you some painkillers before you sleep tonight. Have you been drinking plenty? What have you had?'
Rob told him.
'Well, it's important to drink plenty of water. Have you been emptying your bladder regularly?'
'Yes, no problem,'
'And what about your bowels?'
'No, I haven't been today.'
'Well, don't worry about it. When you've been unconscious for a while, the body kind of shuts down a lot of the normal functions, but you'll soon be back to normal. Don't try and strain. Let's check your blood pressure.'
'Not again,' thought Rob, but sat up in readiness.
'So, are you starting to remember anything more?' Derek asked.

'Only things prior to 1979,' Rob replied. 'And anything anyone has told me today, but nothing of my own from the last forty years. I can't believe I'm sixty years old.'
'Just relax,' Derek said as he started the blood pressure monitor and thrust a thermometer in and out of Rob's ear.
'Can I assume we never had another World War?' Rob asked.
'No ... although we have been involved in a few wars, mostly together with the UN or America. We were on our own with the Falklands War. You don't remember that, do you?'
'We went to war against the Falkland Islands?' Rob asked in amazement.
'No, not against them. The Argentineans invaded and we went over to kick them out. It was a bloody affair, but we did it. I was very young at the time.'
'I'll have to read up about it,' said Rob. 'And what about the Cold War? Is that still going on?'
'No, the Berlin Wall fell in the eighties,' Derek said, looking at Rob's readings.
'Good Heavens!' said Rob. 'Was anyone hurt?'
'When I said the wall fell, I didn't mean literally. I meant they opened up the passage to the West and East Germany is now unified with the rest of Germany. Right, your blood pressure is looking better. When do you normally take your medicines? Mornings or evenings?'
'I've no idea,' said Rob.
'Well, we'll leave the Ramipril to the morning and we'll skip the statins for now. I'll just give you some painkillers before you retire for the night. You've been taking paracetamol up till now, but I'll add some morphine. That will make you a little drowsy but it will help you sleep. In the morning, we'll change your

dressing and make sure there's no sign of infection. I'd better get on with my other patients. I'll see you later.'
Rob still had lots of questions to ask, but Derek had made a start.
While he waited for his hot drink, he had another look at the newspaper and turned to the TV listings. He couldn't believe the number of channels now available. He only knew of three channels – BBC1, BBC2 and ITV. What's more, those three often received interference from foreign stations when certain weather conditions prevailed. Surely all these extra stations were going to interfere with each other. He noticed that some stations were listed under 'Satellite.' He wondered if this was a natural progression of the launch of Telstar back in the sixties. He was very young when that happened, but he had heard about it.
At last the tea trolley arrived and he soon had a steaming mug of drinking chocolate in front of him as he continued reading. The names of the TV programmes meant little to him, but he could see that *Dad's Army* was still going strong. How was it that they could still keep coming up with new story lines?
His hot chocolate had a soporific effect on him and he laid back and fell into a deep sleep. It had been on his mind to avoid sleep in case he didn't wake up again, but he had succumbed. However, after a while, his blissful dreams of a comfortable life in South Luffenham with a comfortable wife were broken by Nurse Jasmine.
'Sorry Robert, you need to take your medication.'
According to Derek, the medication was to help him sleep, so he thought that waking him was daft.
'Can you confirm your name and date of birth?' the pretty young nurse asked.
The same question was asked every time they gave him medication. He assumed this was to ensure that they didn't give the pills to the wrong patient, but she'd

already used his name to waken him. How many Rob Lennards were in this hospital?
Having been disturbed, he was now anxious to return to the land of nod despite his earlier misgivings, but now sleep was elusive. He found the temperature in the hospital too high for his liking and even kicking off one layer of his bed linen didn't help.
When he did eventually nod off, he was woken by an elderly lady screaming in an adjoining ward. 'Help me someone!' she called in a croaky voice, but no one seemed to want to run to her assistance. 'I'm going to shit the bed,' she cried, not caring who could hear. 'Please come! I don't want to shit myself.'
Messing the bed would indeed be embarrassing, but shouting about it was surely equally so. Eventually, someone did go to her and Rob heard some soothing whispers, but ten minutes later, she resumed her distressful cries. This happened several times during the night. Whether she actually soiled her bed, he never knew, but eventually he managed to sleep a little more.

He was woken by the man in the adjoining cubicle pushing back his curtains and visiting the toilet in the corridor opposite. It was daylight. Rob raised his bed so that he could sit up and drink some of his water which by now had become a little warm and tasted the worse for it. After his period of unconsciousness, he wondered if he had slept just the one night, but having found his spectacles, he could see that the newspapers and the water jug were all just as he had left them.
His fellow patient returned and greeted him with a cheerful 'Good morning. Sleep all right?'
'No, not really,' replied Rob.

'No, it's not easy in here,' the man replied. 'Did I hear that you've been having memory problems?'
'You could say that,' said Rob. 'I woke yesterday thinking it was 1979.'
'That's different,' the man said. 'I often forget things, but not forty years. They'll soon sort you out. They're good in here. I've had gall stones – bloody agony, but I'm on the mend. I've been here two weeks. I think I'm going to be released soon for good behaviour. Do you know how long you'll be in here?'
'No, I haven't been told, but I'm waiting for a scan.'
'That will tell them more,' the man said. 'They'll be round with the medication soon. I'm on loads; so is the wife. We both rattle we have so many pills. What about you?'
'I think it's just something for blood pressure and statins.'
'Oh, we all have them.'
Rob wondered if this was what getting old was all about – discussing each other's medication and illnesses.
He took his turn at paying a visit and gazed into the mirror. He didn't like what he saw. Apart from looking so much older and heavier, his jaw was covered in silvery fuzz which seemed to age him still further. He wondered if there was a razor in his belongings. Julie had remembered to bring quite a few things. When he returned to his bed, he would search his cupboard to see what she had brought.
Meanwhile, he was alarmed to see a little blood in his urine. Now he was really worried. That couldn't be normal and his head injury couldn't have caused that. His first thought was of some kind of cancer. He forgot all about searching his cupboard. Instead, he lay on the bed agonising about it until Derek appeared and Rob was able to mention it.

'You had a catheter in earlier, didn't you? That sometimes happens afterwards, but next time you urinate, I'll give you a bottle and we'll get it tested. I'm sure it's normal.'
That was a relief. Now all he had to worry about was regaining those lost forty years.
Derek visited the man next door. 'Hello Les. How are you?'
'I think I'm getting stir crazy. Any idea when I can leave?'
'Ask the doctors when they come around,' Derek replied.
'I have done. I never get a straight answer,' Les said.
Later, after Derek had moved on, Les said to Rob 'I'm just going down to get myself a newspaper. Do you need anything?'
'No, I've still got yesterday's *Telegraph* to read, thank you.'
'It'll be time for breakfast when I come back,' Les said as he started to walk away. 'I look forward to my porridge.'
As Rob's second newspaper was a broadsheet, he decided that it would be easier to read sitting in his chair. As he wandered through the pages, he still found it all confusing. He recognised none of the politicians; the business pages talked about companies that he'd never heard of and it was full of words that were new to him, such as this *Brexit* and the *Euro*. He decided to ask Les a few questions when he returned. He seemed like a friendly and intelligent chap.
Before he could do that, breakfast arrived and with it, a fresh jug of water. Rob's toast and cup of tea were both a little on the cold side and seeing Les enjoying his porridge made him think that perhaps he had chosen the wrong items from the sparse breakfast menu, but the lunch options looked more appetising.

He waited until Les had finished his meal before diving in with his enquiries. 'Can you explain to me what this Brexit is?' he asked.
Les laughed. 'You want me to explain Brexit. I need someone to tell me what's going on.' He looked at Rob for a minute before trying. 'Well ... back in 2016, we had a referendum which asked the British public if they wanted to stay in the EU or leave. I don't suppose you remember, do you?'
'No,' said Rob. 'What's the EU?'
Les laughed again. 'That's another good question. Do you know about the Common Market?' Rob nodded. 'Well, it's grown out of that, but it's no longer just about trading with each other. It's now all about political union. There are now over twenty countries in the EU and we can trade with any of them without worrying about tariffs, which is good, but we don't have a free rein to trade with other countries like Australia, Canada or America for instance. And there's a European parliament which we can vote for. Sounds all right, doesn't it?'
Rob suspected that there was a big 'but' coming and wasn't sure how to respond, so he didn't.
Les continued. 'But the people who make all the decisions are unelected. The MEPs - the ones that we vote in – well, I don't really know what they do. For the last two to three years, our leaders have been negotiating with their unelected bureaucrats for a deal to leave and we've been getting nowhere – because they don't really want us to go, otherwise other countries might want to leave as well. Mind you, I'm sure our leaders don't want us to either. As you may have guessed, I voted to leave. My wife, bless her heart, voted to remain – and that's typical of the country as a whole. Almost half the country want to remain, but

the majority voted 'leave.' I don't suppose you know what you did?'
'I've absolutely no idea,' Rob replied. 'I don't really do politics.'
'Nor do I really, but this is important ...'
Before he could continue, a nurse arrived with a cheery 'Good morning.'
'Morning Gorgeous,' Les said. 'How's my favourite nurse, this morning.'
'I don't know,' said the nurse. 'What's her name? Are you going on about politics again? You know it upsets your blood pressure. I'd better check it if you don't mind.'
'Well it always goes up when you're around,' he said offering her his arm.
Rob guessed he would have to leave his questioning for a little while.
As he returned to his newspaper, he heard his 'phone ringing. It was still plugged into its charger on the other side of the bed. As he approached it, he could see the word 'JOOLS' in the middle of the screen. He had no idea what that meant ... and how did he answer it? There was no visible mouthpiece or cradle like the 'phones to which he was accustomed. He picked it up and said 'hello' but it continued ringing. He remembered that when his wife answered her 'phone, she had touched the screen. He tried that. The ringing stopped. Had he broken something?
'Hello,' a female voice called from within the device. He put it to his ear as he had done before.
'Hello,' he said tentatively.
'Rob? It's me, love. Are you there?'
'Yes, I'm here,' he replied, realising that it was his wife, but not showing any great emotion.
'How are you? Is there any improvement?'

'My head feels a little better, but I still can't remember anything.'
'Oh dear ... never mind. Look ... I can't make it to the afternoon visitors' session. I have to work all day, but I will be there in the evening, I promise you. Sarah said she would like to join me if she can get a babysitter. I can't talk for long just now. I have a meeting I have to attend. I will see you tonight. Give me a call if there's any news. Bye for now.'
'Bye,' he replied and the 'phone went quiet. He didn't know how to put the 'phone back on its non-existent cradle so he laid it down where he had found it, still attached to the charger.
He sat down on the bed feeling strangely disappointed that she wouldn't be visiting that afternoon and wondered why that should be the case. He hardly knew her but he wanted to see her again. Was she just a female substitute for his precious Kate? Perhaps he was just anxious to find out about his new life and move on from his past. There was also a little nervousness about possibly meeting his daughter 'for the first time.'
He looked for his newspaper again, but before he could pick it up, he was approached by the friendly nurse who had handled Les with such aplomb.
'Hello,' she said with a delightful smile that would make any patient feel better. 'I'm Sharon. I need to take your blood pressure and temperature and then we'll see about your medication. I hope you're not as much trouble as that reprobate in the next bed.'
Rob smiled. 'I won't give you any trouble ... and don't take any notice of Les. He was flirting with Derek last night.'
'Hey! I heard that!' Les said feigning indignation. 'I'm not like that – not these days anyhow.'
As Sharon took his blood pressure, she said 'We're going to change your dressing this morning – and then

we'll have a look to make sure there's no sign of infection. How does it feel?'
'It's feeling a little better all the time, but my memory is still the same.'
'Yes, Derek was telling me about that. It's most unusual; at least, I've never come across a case like it, but time will tell.'
'I was told I would be having a scan. Do you know when?' Rob asked.
'No, they're very busy. You might have to come back as an outpatient. Where do you live – or don't you know?'
'I live in South Luffenham, but I've no idea where that is.'
'Oh, I do. It's a nice village – got a nice pub. I went there last year when the Uppingham Jazz and Soul Band were playing outside. We had a lovely barbeque. Or was that North Luffenham? No, I think that might have been North Luffenham, but they're both nice places. Your pressure and temperature look fine. I'll fetch your medication.'
She returned a few minutes later and asked 'What's your name and date of birth?'
He was tempted to say 'John Wayne' or something facetious but decided against it. Would anyone still know who John Wayne was?
'Here is your ramipril and a couple more paracetamol. Keep drinking plenty of water.'
Rob wanted to ask Les a few more questions about the state of the world, but he could see that his neighbour was engrossed in his newspaper and decided to read his own some more. The other topic that cropped up in several articles was *climate change*. Some experts seemed to be saying that everyone has to change their way of life. Who are all these experts and what are they expert in? It seemed as though in many respects, the world had not changed for the better in forty years.

He couldn't see any articles relating to colonies on Mars nor even the moon.
He decided to give up on reading and turned to the crossword. Julie said he now enjoyed doing the *Telegraph* cryptic crossword, but he wasn't sure what that meant. He read the first clue – *I came in Latin Church for an Italian city.*
That didn't make any sense. It wasn't grammatical. He thought of some Italian cities that were six letters long – Verona, perhaps? Naples? Venice? But where does a Latin church come into that? Italy is Roman Catholic, so they could all have Latin churches. He looked at some more clues and none of them were any clearer. He gave up and fell back on his bed. Whenever he lay back on his bed, his thoughts turned to Kate and once again his stomach clenched up. The paracetamol didn't seem to help his heartache.

Chapter 5

After what seemed like a very long morning, the doctors finally paid Rob a visit. His bed was at the end of that part of the ward and he was usually the last to be seen by anyone. The previous day's dark skinned lady with a laptop was with them, but he wasn't sure if he had seen any of the others before. The one who looked like the most senior had a slight West Indian accent.
'Mr ... Lennard, is it? Ma name is Jason – Senior Consultant. How are you?' He was looking at Rob's notes as he spoke and not looking at his patient at all.
'I'm getting better, thank you, but my memory is still stuck in 1979.'
'Mmm, I dink we'll have a look at your wound.'
One of his assistants pointed to something in Rob's notes.
'Oh, I see you had the dressin' changed dis mornin' and there was no sign of infection and your blood tests confirm that, so we'll leave dat for now.'
He carried on looking at the notes a little longer. 'I don't see any reason for you to remain here. I'm sure you'd rather be at home. I'll arrange for you to be discharged. You will need your dressin' changed regularly. Yo' G.P. can do that.'
'What about my memory?' Rob asked.
'Mmm, yes dat is a concern, but layin' here isn't going to solve dee problem. You might start remembering tings tomorrow or next week. We don't know how long it will take. Perhaps some kind of regression therapy might help. Meanwhile, we'll see you as an outpatient in about a week. You mustn't drive in between time. Do you have someone to take you home?'

'Probably my wife,' Rob replied. He would be glad to leave but was still a little anxious that he didn't have a solution to his problem.
The doctor turned to one of his assistants and asked 'Can you arrange the discharge, please?'
'Sounds like you're going to beat me out of here,' said Les after the doctors had moved on. 'I'd like to have seen how you get on with your memory problem, but I'm sure you'd rather be at home.'
'Yes,' said Rob, thinking that he knew nothing about his home. 'I'm wondering if someone should be contacting my wife to pick me up.'
'I wouldn't hurry her. It takes them ages to discharge people. There was a chap last week was told in the morning he would be leaving – just like you – and it was nine o'clock in the evening before he finally left. I'd give her a call anyway ... just to give her the good news.'
'Yes, I should,' said Rob, except that he didn't know how to call someone.
'I don't know her number,' he said.
'It will be in your *contacts,*' Les said.
Rob gave him a puzzled look.
'Give me your 'phone,' Les said.
Rob fetched it, disconnecting the charger as he did so, hoping that was not going to cause a problem.
'Right,' said Les, finding an icon for *contacts.* 'You press this to bring up all the contacts on your 'phone and then you scroll down to find her name, which is?'
'Julie,' replied Rob not understanding how just brushing a screen with your fingers was going to help.
'There's no one named Julie here. Do you have a nickname for her? Like Snugglebums, for instance?'
'Is that what you call your wife?' Rob said.
'You don't want to know what I call the old ... how about JOOLS? Could that be her?'

Rob remembered that name coming up when she called earlier.
'Yes, that's probably her,' he replied.
'Shall we call her?' Les asked.
'I guess so,' said Rob.
'It's ringing,' said Les and handed over the device.
'Rob? Is everything all right?' a voice said.
'Yes ... I'm calling because I've just had a visit from the doctors and they want to discharge me. Can you come and fetch me later?'
'Did they tell you when?'
'No, but the chap in the next bed told me that last week a chap was told he would be discharged in the morning and by the time they sorted out the paperwork and everything, he eventually left about nine at night, so I don't think there's any hurry.'
He could hear Julie sighing and presumably thinking. 'I could come now, but that doesn't sound like it would be any use. As I told you earlier, I have a meeting this afternoon that I really need to attend. I doubt whether I will be finished before five thirty. If that's a problem, you'll have to let me know. What else did they say?'
'They want me to come back for an outpatient appointment in about a week.'
'That's okay,' Julie said. 'Anything about your head and memory?'
'The head is healing and there's no sign of infection – and they don't think my memory is going to get any better by being in hospital. That makes sense to me – and I'm bored stiff.'
'Was this the same doctor I saw yesterday?' she asked.
'No, this was a coloured doctor.'
'You can't say *coloured*!' she said abruptly.
'Why not?'

'It can cause offence. You must say *black* or West Indian ... or Afro Caribbean; but never *coloured*. Some people take offence.'
Rob didn't understand. He always thought the term was less offensive than others he might have used. 'Is this the same people who have endured hundreds of years of slavery, apartheid and civil rights issues? And now the term *coloured* offends them?'
'I can't explain it all now,' she said, 'but be careful of what you say to anyone. If a woman talks about her wife; or a man talks about his husband, try not to act shocked. And just to warn you, if you say anything remotely homophobic, the police might arrest you for a hate crime.'
'Have I woken up in 2019 or 1984?' he said.
'We've had this discussion before,' she said. 'Just be careful. Whatever you do, don't use *Eenie Meenie Miney Mo* for making a selection. I'll see you later.'
Rob decided that life in 1979 was far less complicated.
He told Les what his wife had just told him. Les sympathised with Rob's dilemma, being of an age when people were less sensitive about such matters and had other things to worry about.
They continued talking for a while and at last, Rob discovered the story behind the Euro, complete with Les' take on the subject. They also discussed space travel in the last forty years and climate change. All of this was most enlightening, but Rob still hadn't recovered his memory by lunchtime.

Just before lunch, Nurse Sharon re-appeared. 'Was it something I said?' she asked of Rob.
'Pardon?' Rob replied.
'I hear you're leaving us already.'

'Oh, yes,' Rob replied. 'No, it's certainly nothing personal, but I will be glad to leave. Do you know when I'll be able to go?'
'Not just yet. They're still sorting out your appointment – and your scan. Have you arranged your transport yet?'
'I rang my wife. She won't be here before five thirty. Do you think that will be all right?'
'I'm sure it will,' she replied with a delightful smile. 'You might as well have your tea before you leave.'

Rob knew that it would seem like an age before his wife arrived and he had read as much of the newspaper as he was going to. How else to while away the next few hours? He had one thought.
After he had demolished his lunch which was completed by tasty apple pie and custard, he sat down with his 'phone. He knew that the afternoon visitors would soon be arriving and from experience, the nursing staff tended to keep out of their way. All the other patients were likely to receive visitors so it was essential that Rob had something with which to occupy himself to stop him looking like Billy No-mates.
He found a button on the side of the device which caused it to spring into life just as he'd seen Les do earlier. There on the small screen were two words – *Menu* and *Contacts.* Underneath each was a button. He would start with the contacts. Sure enough, there was a long list of peoples' names. Les had moved his fingers down the screen and Rob now did likewise. This seemed like magic to him and he was fascinated by the action. Then he started looking at the names in more detail. They were helpfully in alphabetical order. He had no idea who Anne G. might be. He touched the name and her phone number appeared. He was none the

wiser. He eventually found an arrow that took him back to the list.
There was a Ben. That must be his son to whom he had spoken the day before. Rob knew that Ben still lived in Norfolk, but the number began 01553, He thought all '01' numbers indicated the London area. King's Lynn was 0553 wasn't it? Perhaps the number had been set up incorrectly. He was tempted to ring the number, but he remembered Julie saying he had a 'pay-as-you-go' phone and King's Lynn was probably a long distance call.
Then he noticed another name – 'Ben Mobile.' So Ben had an old-fashioned British Telecomm telephone as well as a mobile.
As he continued to amuse himself by studying his 'contact' list, the visitors started arriving. On other occasions when this happened, he felt awkward at being on his own but he was determined that his mobile 'phone would ease that situation. However, he was taken by surprise when a tall attractive young lady appeared, saying 'There you are!'
She looked strangely familiar and at first, he thought she must be one of the doctors who had attended the rounds the previous day, but when she leaned over and kissed his forehead, he decided that would be highly unlikely.
'How are you feeling, now?' she asked. He hesitated and before he could answer, she added 'I was going to come with mum this evening, but she said you might be leaving later, so I thought I'd come and see if I can prepare the way.'
'You're Sarah,' he said, feeling pleased with himself for remembering her name. Of course, that was why she looked vaguely familiar. She had her mother's eyes and stature. In fact, she may have been an inch or two taller. Her bosom was a little lighter than her mother's

but still impressive – and she was gorgeous. Could he really have produced such a lovely daughter?
'You do recognise me. Mum said you wouldn't.'
'No, I'm sorry,' he said. 'I don't recognise you, but you mentioned your mum, so it had to be you. You got a babysitter, then?'
'Oh, the children are at school – playschool in the case of Belinda. She's only three.'
'I'm looking forward to meeting them – I mean seeing them again,' he said thinking that sounded better. 'If they are as lovely as their mother, they must be gorgeous. I can't believe I fathered someone so lovely.'
He wondered if this sounded a little creepy but it was what he was thinking. He still thought of himself as twenty years old and she was clearly a little older than that.
'Have you been making 'phone calls?' she asked, seeing him holding his mobile.
'No, I was just looking at my contacts to see if I recognised anyone's name.'
'And did you?'
'So far, only Ben, but I hadn't finished. I was wondering if my parents were in the list.' They hadn't been connected to the 'phone in 1979 so he wasn't expecting to find their number.
Sarah placed her hand on his. 'Nanny passed away a couple of years ago. She went in her sleep and Grandpa a few years earlier. I'm sorry.'
Rob closed his eyes trying not to weep. He felt the need to make a good impression on this new stranger in his life and he didn't think that crying would help his cause. 'I bet so many people have gone in the last forty years.' He realised that she was still standing up. 'Here sit on this chair. I'll sit on my bed.'
He moved around her carefully so as to not expose his rear view.

'I'm glad to see you,' he said. 'I was only looking at my 'phone to occupy my time. I've read the papers. I could do with a book.'
'You've got your Kindle on top of your cupboard,' she said. 'That will have plenty of things on it.' Then she gave a little laugh. 'You've probably read most things on there but you won't remember having done so.'
'What is it – this Kindle?'
She spent the next few minutes demonstrating it. 'I think your favourite author was Patrick O'Brian. You could wade through those, starting with *Master and Commander*.'
'I was never much of one for reading,' he said.
'What?' she said. 'You're always reading.'
'I suppose I must have changed a lot in forty years. Your mother said I enjoy doing cryptic cross words, but I picked up this one,' he reached for his newspaper, 'and I couldn't make sense of it. *I came in Latin Church for an Italian city.* What on Earth does that mean? It's not even proper English.'
'Let me have a look,' she said, taking the paper from him. 'Yes, it's *Venice*. You have to break it down. Look, *I came in Latin* is *Veni*, as in I came, I saw, I conquered. *Church* is CE as in Church of England and Venice is an Italian city.'
'I did think of Venice,' he said, 'but I couldn't see why; now I do. You're clever. Do you take after me or your mother?'
'I think it's just a question of how you think about it, but we often used to do these crosswords together. You probably taught me. Try this one – two down. You've got the first letter 'E.' It's four letters – *A cheese made backwards.'*
He was still struggling.
'Think of the word *made,*' she said, 'and then read it backwards.

'Edam,' he said. 'What's that?'
'It's a cheese; a Dutch cheese.'
'I've heard of Dutch cheese,' he said. 'That's the one with red rind, but we never called it Edam. I'm learning something new here. Well, now I've got a couple of things to occupy me – this and the Kindle ... and just as I'm about to be discharged. So, if you want other books to read on a Kindle, do you buy another Kindle with a different selection?'
Sarah laughed. 'Of course not! You download them onto this one.'
He looked blank. 'Er ... download them?'
'From the internet, Dad. I'd show you, but we probably don't have a Wi-Fi connection here.'
'The internet? Wi-Fi?' he asked.
'Oh dear,' she sighed. 'I'll let mum explain that when you get home. You've got a good connection at home.'
He resisted the urge to ask what she meant by 'connection.'
'I hope I recover my memory soon,' he said. 'I want the memories of seeing you and Ben growing up. Can I ask how old you both are?'
'I'm twenty-nine and Ben's thirty two,' she replied.
'Are you a full time mum?' he asked.
'No, I work part time – thirty hours a week. Belinda goes to a pre-school nursery Monday to Thursday, but not Fridays so I always keep that free for her – and Barney was the same up until this year when he went into the main school. The two schools are part of the same complex in Ketton. We have a very good relationship with the nursery assistants there. They are excellent and always get a good review from Ofsted.'
'Ofsted?' Rob asked.
'This is too much like hard work,' she said with a laugh.
'What work do you do?' Rob asked.
'I'm an auditor,' she replied.

'Is that like checking up on accounts and so on?' he asked.
'Oh, no. We use an outside organisation to do that. No, this is checking that everyone in the business conforms to the work practices that have been laid down – internal procedures and standards; that sort of thing.'
'I've never heard of such a thing,' he replied, 'but then I seem to be in the dark over so many things. It makes me feel quite ignorant.'
'Oh, Dad, you're not ignorant. You're very intelligent. You always win at *Trivial Pursuit* – that's a board game we play as a family, before you ask.'
'What does your husband do for a living?' Rob asked.
'He's a plumber. He's mainly self-employed, but he also does some work for a company called City Plumbers, based here in Peterborough; that way he can do a few jobs for them and earn money, but his own work isn't enough for him to have to be VAT registered. That saves a lot of paperwork and he can undercut bigger plumbers. You know about VAT don't you?'
'Yes, Value Added Tax. It replaced Purchase Tax. It's ten per cent isn't it?'
'And the rest,' she said. 'I think it's twenty per cent now. That's a lot to add to a bill.'
'I bet he's popular among your friends and neighbours,' Rob said.
'He's not always popular with the neighbours when he parks his van in the road. There's only room for one vehicle in our drive and I need to park my car somewhere.'
'What car do you drive?' he asked.
'It's a Qashqai ... a Nissan.' She added the last bit when she saw his puzzled look.
'Oh, that's Datsun, isn't it?' he said 'I've got a Datsun Sunny. My first car was an Allegro but it kept breaking

down. The Jap cars are so much more reliable. Mine came with a built in radio.'
'You haven't got a Sunny, Dad. You've got a Skoda now.'
'No! Have I sunk so low as to buy a Skoda? They're the worst cars you can buy. They have a terrible reputation like all the Iron Curtain cars. Doors fall off and they are the butt of so many jokes. Why do Skodas have a heated rear window? So that you keep your hands warm when you're pushing it. A chap goes into a garage and asks if he can have wing mirror for his Skoda. The garage owner says "*That sounds like a good swap.*"
'Oh, Dad. Skodas aren't like that anymore. They're basically VWs now. You're very pleased with yours.'
He sighed. 'I've still got so many questions going around my head. I hope you don't mind me questioning you.'
'Of course not,' she replied. 'But is it helping you to remember things?'
'No, I'm afraid not, but at least I'm starting to build a picture of my new life.'
They continued talking for a while longer, but eventually, Sarah said 'I'm going to have to leave you now. I have to pick up the children from school. Ketton is about twenty minutes from here and I mustn't be late. I have to park my car at home first. It's mayhem when all the other mothers arrive in their four-by-fours to pick up their kids from school. We always insist that they walk to and from school.'
'I always walked to school,' Rob said. 'We didn't have a choice.'
'I'll see you soon,' Sarah said leaning over to kiss his forehead. 'I think you need a shave and a shower. 'Bye for now.'

‘I’ll look forward to seeing you again soon,’ Rob said as she turned the corner and he really meant it. He felt really proud to be the father of such a charming woman. She was not only very good looking, she was intelligent and had a very kind and caring nature. He didn’t resent her parting comment about needing a shower because it was true. There was a shower in the toilet but he thought it would be awkward with his head bandaged.

Chapter 6

Sarah had left before the end of visiting hours and there were still a few visitors hanging around some of the other patients, so Rob pulled his curtains about his bed to give himself some privacy while he knelt down to examine the contents of his bedside cupboard. He was hoping that Julie might have brought some toiletries, but all he found were some clothes which he didn't recognise as belonging to him. He wouldn't have been seen dead in these as a twenty year old. In 1979, he wore trousers with a thirty two inch waist. The ones in his cupboard said thirty six, but they looked about the right length.

He removed his gown and tried on the underpants and trousers and was surprised that they did fit, as did the uninspiring plain shirt, all of which was in contrast to the colourful patterned shirts and flared trousers he was used to. Perhaps these clothes were now fashionable he thought as he finished dressing. A spot of blood on the collar of his shirt led him to believe that this was what he was wearing at the time of his accident and would suffice for his journey home. More to the point, he could now wander across to the toilet without showing off his rear quarters to the world.

Inside the toilet, there didn't appear to be any soap in the washbasin, but there was an anti-bacterial foam dispenser. He undid his shirt and did his best to wash his face and torso without the use of a flannel or a sponge and then applied some of the foam to his armpits. He then used several paper towels to dry himself. At least this would mask his body odour for a while, but he still had grey fuzz around his chin.

As he returned to his bed, he could see the last of the visitors departing and the two nurses returning to their

duty. The man in the bed opposite was already on his 'phone telling someone that he hoped to be home by the weekend.
Les addressed Rob. 'Getting ready to go home, young man?' Rob was used to be addressed as such but realised that in this case. Les was being ironic.
'Er ... yeah ... I still don't know when, though,' he replied.
They were interrupted by Nurse Sharon telling Les that she needed to check his blood pressure again. The second nurse, who had not previously spoken to Rob and did not introduce herself, followed Sharon to speak to Rob. 'We've got your discharge papers here and the remains of the medication which you brought with you. There's some paracetamol in case you still have any pain. We've also got your appointment next week at the Ambulatory Building. Do you know where that is?'
'I don't even know where I am now,' he replied with a smile.
'Well, when you go out the main entrance, you turn right and keep following the building round. There is another car park nearer to that building but it fills up fast. Have you got someone to take you home?'
'My wife will be along a little later,' Rob replied. 'It's all right for me to wait here, isn't it?'
'Yes, of course. Do you have any questions?'
'What about my scan?' Rob asked.
'Scan?' the nurse said with a puzzled look on her face.
'I was told I would have a scan,' Rob said.
'Who told you that?' she asked.
'I can't remember,' he replied, trying to think when that was.
'Do you know anything about a scan, Sharon?' the nurse asked.
'They said you don't need a scan,' Sharon replied. 'You've no sign of concussion now, but if you feel light

headed or sick at anytime, contact your GP immediately.'
'Okay,' Rob responded. 'What about my bandages?'
'You'll need to have them changed regularly,' said the young nurse. 'Your GP will do that. You're with the Uppingham Surgery aren't you?'
'I've no idea,' Rob replied. 'I don't remember the last time I saw a doctor.'
'Your wife will know, I expect,' the nurse replied.

Julie hadn't arrived by the time Rob's meal was served up. He felt awkward sitting there in his civvies waiting to be taken home. He was no longer a patient and had no right to occupy a bed.
Visiting time came and there was still no sign of his wife. At twenty five minutes past six, she arrived. 'Bloody HR!' she said throwing her handbag on his bed. 'I'm sure the world would be a better place without HR. Sorry Love. I got here as soon as I could. I've had nothing to eat except a sandwich at lunchtime. Have you eaten?'
'Yes, I ate about five o'clock. What's HR?'
'Of course, HR hadn't been invented in 1979 ... bloody good job, too. It stands for Human Resources and it's growing like a plague. They cover hiring and firing, sickness and absence, terms and conditions ... benefits ... union negotiations ... and anything else they chose. Do you know, a few years ago when there was a bit of a recession, every part of the company had to cut costs and even lose a few staff. HR took on more people. You never hear of HR staff being made redundant. How are you, anyway? Sorry - I should have asked.'
'I'm all right, thank you,' he replied. 'I had a visit from Sarah. That cheered me up. She's a lovely girl. I can't believe she's my daughter.'

‘I can assure you that she is,’ said Julie. ‘There is no doubt about that – and Ben and all the grandchildren are lovely, too. Now, you look as if you’re all ready to go.’
‘Yes, I think so. I’ve got my discharge paper and a letter about my appointment next week, but as I can’t drive for a while, you’ll have to bring me. I also need to have my dressing changed regularly. The nurse said our GP can do that.’
‘Fat chance!’ said Julie. ‘I’ll phone them and see if the nurse can change it, but even that needs several days notice. What about this scan?’
‘They say I don’t need one,’ Rob replied.
Julie’s face took on an air of obvious impatience. ‘We need to find out what’s wrong with your memory ... and you were unconscious for the best part of two days. Who can I talk to?’
‘They don’t think the memory is anything to do with the knock on the head,’ he said.
‘Nonsense! That’s too big a coincidence in my book.’
‘Can’t we just see what they say next week?’ said Rob, realising that as the man in this relationship, he should be the masterful one, except that he felt a little overawed by his more worldly wife. ‘If we try and find a doctor now, we’ll be here all night. I’m looking forward to seeing my new home.’
‘All right,’ Julie said. ‘I must admit I’m a little worked up after that meeting I just left – and I’m very hungry. Do you mind if we pop over to the supermarket to get something? Now do you have everything?’
As Rob stood up, she gave him a big hug. Despite the fact that she was his wife, he didn’t feel that he knew her well enough to respond with any fervour, but he placed his hands on her shoulders and it felt nice. ‘I’ll be glad when we all get back to normal,’ she said. ‘We’ll get you sorted out.’

As they parted, his thoughts turned (and not for the first time) to their possible sex life. Did people have sex in their fifties and sixties?
They both picked up their belongings and headed along the corridor, passing a group of nurses which included Nurse Sharon. 'Are you off?' she asked, although the reply was going to be obvious.
'Yes. Thank you for looking after me,' Rob said. 'And pass on my thanks to everyone else.'
'You're welcome,' Sharon said.
'Are you on Trip Advisor?' Julie asked and received a polite laugh in return.
'What's Trip ...?' Rob started to ask, but Julie stopped him and told him she'd explain it later.
As they followed the "Way out" signs, Julie asked 'Are you going to be all right with the stairs or do you want to use the lift?'
'Stairs,' he replied, thinking she was being over protective of his condition. But when he took his first few steps down the stairs, he realised that his knees and hips were a little stiffer than he was used to and he was more aware of the extra weight he was carrying. Looking down at his feet made him feel a little dizzy.
When they reached the atrium at the bottom of the stairs, Julie said 'I just need to pay for the car park' and she led them towards a ticket machine.
'Do you have to pay to park at the hospital?' Rob asked, following her like a puppy.
'Even the people who work here have to pay,' she replied. 'I've spent a small fortune on parking this week.'
He watched her as she pushed a ticket into the slot and then proceeded to use a debit card which required her to enter a pin number. 'Don't you have to put some coins in?' he asked.

‘I could do, but who carries two pounds ninety in cash?’ she replied. ‘And it doesn’t give change.’
‘Two pounds ninety?’ he said in disbelief.
‘It was six pounds on Sunday when you were still unconscious,’ she said.
Rob realised that in the course of forty years, inflation was bound to have been a big factor, but he couldn’t believe that Julie needed to pay six pounds just to park her car at a hospital.
Julie retrieved her ticket and debit card and they headed out of the entrance doors.
‘Have you brought the Skoda?’ he asked, looking around at the large car park, not recognising any models at all.
‘No, I’ve got my car,’ she said.
‘Do we have two cars, then?’ he asked.
‘Of course. You can’t rely on public transport in Rutland. There is a bus that goes between Stamford and Uppingham, but it’s every two hours and it goes around all the villages. I’ve used it a couple of times when I had to – and it’s painful.’
Julie’s vehicle was way over the other side of the huge car park and, as it was still quite light, Rob couldn’t help stopping every now and then to look at another unfamiliar car. He said ‘A lot of these cars look like vans with windows. Why do people need such big cars these days?’
‘It’s the fashion. They’re called SUVs – sports utility vehicles. Many of them are four wheel drive; often driven by women.’
‘But aren’t they expensive?’ Rob asked.
‘Yes, but they’re probably paid for on a lease agreement, so the drivers don’t actually own them – and it’s a big status symbol to drop your children off at school in one of those.’

‘I don’t see any Austins or Hillmans – nor even Rovers,’ Rob said.
‘There’s no such thing now. It’s a long story. We still make cars in this country, but they are mostly foreign owned. Even Rolls Royce is owned by a German company. This is mine,’ she said as she opened the door locks remotely.
Rob approached it from behind. ‘A Toyota Hybrid. That’s a funny name.’
‘It’s actually an Auris. Hybrid means it runs on battery power as well as petrol. It makes it very economical.’
‘Like a milk float,’ he said.
‘No, not like a milk float!’
Rob was surprised to see Julie entering the car without unlocking the door with a key. He followed her lead and sat beside her. ‘Did you leave this unlocked while you were in the hospital?’
‘No, of course not! I just unlocked it with a remote control.’
Once again, Rob was impressed with modern technology, but was disappointed that they couldn’t just beam themselves into their home.
‘Have you got a television in here?’ he asked looking at the screen next to the dials and switches in front of him.
‘No, you wouldn’t be allowed to watch TV while you’re driving, but just keep looking at the screen if you want to be impressed.’
She put the car into reverse gear and an image appeared on the screen.
‘What’s that?’ he asked.
‘That’s the view behind so that I can see that it’s safe to reverse.’
‘So you have a camera strapped to the back?’ he asked.

‘I wouldn’t say strapped. There is a very small camera, though – and at night it copes with poor lighting conditions.’
As she pulled away, the image changed to a map. Rob decided not to make comment about it. He realised that perhaps he was starting to sound like an idiot questioning every new piece of modern technology, but that didn’t prevent him from being impressed as he watched the display alter to reflect their progress from the car park to the road.
‘Bloody dipstick,’ she said as a young man in a souped up Corsa overtook her on the inside and ground to a sudden halt at the traffic lights.
‘Traffic lights on a roundabout,’ said Rob. ‘I’ve never seen such a thing. There’s nothing coming and we all have to wait for the lights to change.’
‘It gets very busy during the rush hour,’ Julie said. ‘They need them then, but I don’t understand why they can’t be switched off at other times.’ To prove her point, they had to stop again halfway around the roundabout.
As they eventually moved off, Rob couldn’t help himself. He had to ask. ‘How does this work, then?’
‘What? Oh, the Satnav. Don’t ask me exactly how it works, but basically, it tracks our position from satellites and plots it into the maps. If you enter your destination, it will give you annoying instructions how to get there. You always insist on using an atlas if we go somewhere unfamiliar.’
‘I see,’ he said, not wanting to ask any more questions just then, except that when they pulled into the supermarket’s car park, he said ‘I’ve never seen such a big supermarket. How much do you have to pay to park here?’
‘You don’t have to pay, here,’ she said.
‘So you pay to park at a hospital, but not to park here. That doesn’t make sense to me.’

Even though it was now the evening, there were still a lot of people milling about. In his experience most people did their shopping on a Saturday. As they entered the building, he was amazed at the size of the place and couldn't understand how people knew where to go to find things. He wondered how many young children got lost there. However, Julie was familiar with the layout and led him towards the in-store cafe.
'I'm starving,' she said. 'I hope I can still get a good meal.' But she was disappointed to find that the cafe had just closed. 'Damn, I really fancied a breakfast. Shall we get a ready meal?'
'Whatever you feel,' Rob responded, not knowing what a ready meal was.
'What time did you eat?' she asked.
'About five o'clock,' he replied.
'Can you manage to share an Indian?'
'I've never had an Indian,' he said.
She sighed. 'Of course you have. You love an Indian. I'll get a couple of different meals and we can share each other's.' She knew exactly where to go in this huge building to find what she wanted and picked up some milk as well. Rob wasn't sure that he wanted to drink milk from a plastic container, but he said nothing.
Julie found her way to a self-checkout machine while Rob watched open-mouthed. Had the world become so honest, that shoppers were now trusted to make their own payments? Somehow, he doubted it.
As they headed home, she asked 'Has anything that's happened today struck a chord with you at all?'
'No, I'm afraid not.'
'I've had a thought about this,' she said. 'Did something happen in 1979 that is relevant to your condition?'
'If it did, I don't know what,' he replied. 'Maybe, it was something soon after the point that I remember. I

wonder if there's anyone who knew me then who could help. I understand both of my parents are dead, but what about my brother Ken? Do you ever see him?'
'Ken has been living in Canada for many years. You told me that he was getting very despondent about all the civil unrest in the country at that time - the miners' strike and the battles with the police and everything else that was happening around then. He left before we got married so I don't really know him.'
'Yes, I remember him having strong views on everything. When our old Grammar School in Lynn became a comprehensive, he was almost in tears. He said it was the thin end of the wedge.'
'I hear the school is very badly rated these days,' said Julie. 'Anyway, we've never really kept in touch. We don't even receive a Christmas card anymore.'
'So I've got no family,' Rob said with a sigh.
'Scuse me!' Julie said. 'You've got a very good family – me, two children and three grandchildren!'
'Yes, of course. I meant none of the family that I grew up with. I dare say all my aunts and uncles have gone.'
'And you haven't kept in touch with any cousins as far as I know, so it would be very hard to find them now. We could try your brother on Facebook again, but you have already tried once before. I'll tell you all about Facebook another time.' He had been about to query it before she stopped him.
As they drove along the A47, he asked 'What's that river?'
'That's the Nene. We've had some very pleasant walks along the Nene – a bit further upstream, around Oundle and Wadenhoe.'
'It goes through Wisbech doesn't it?' he asked. 'I've been to Wisbech a few times but never to Peterborough.'

'Well, obviously, you have,' she said. 'You just don't remember.'
'Yes, that's what I meant.'
A few miles later, they passed the water mill at Duddington. 'Is that still the Nene?' he asked.
'No, that's the Welland. It goes through Stamford and Spalding.' She was starting to sound a little impatient and he wondered if he was sounding like an inquisitive child, but how was he to learn about his new environment unless he asked questions.
He was still being fascinated by the Satnav and how it kept up with their progress. 'You don't appear to have a radio,' he said. 'Nor a cassette player.'
'Nobody uses cassettes anymore,' she said, 'And most new cars don't even come with a CD player, but there is a radio' and to prove the point, she pressed a button and Rutland Radio came on, playing an old Commodores song.
Rob recognised it and started singing along, but his singing voice sounded deeper than he remembered and he felt self-conscious so ceased after a few bars.
'We now load all your old CDs onto a card so we don't have to carry them around in the car,' she said and realising that this was beyond his comprehension, she added 'I will explain CDs and cards to you at some point, but not just now. I want to get home and microwave this meal.'
A few minutes later, they pulled into their drive and she parked next to Rob's Skoda. 'This is home,' she announced.

Chapter 7

'I think you should have a shave and a shower while I prepare this meal,' said Julie as they entered their house. Ron really wanted to explore the house and garden. After all, this was the home that he now owned, presumably jointly with his wife. The cramped home he remembered from 1979 was his parents' and one for which he had no responsibility. But if his wife was going to be preparing their meal, it made sense for him to clean himself up a little.
'You'll have to show me where the bathroom is,' he said.

A little later, he rejoined his wife feeling remarkably refreshed and clean-shaven. 'I couldn't wash my hair because of the bandage but that's the best shave I've ever had,' he said. 'Five blades in that razor! It's a lovely bathroom. I like the tiles.' He was really just making small talk as he felt a little uncomfortable in his strange surroundings.
'Well, you did the tiling, so you ought to like them,' she said.
'I did the tiling?' He'd never done anything like that in his early twenty year old life. His parents' house didn't even have bathroom tiles.
'I helped you choose them, of course,' she said. 'You used YouTube for some tips about the task.'
'What's You...'
'All in good time,' she said. 'This meal is all ready, so sit down and enjoy it.'
He did as he was told. They were eating in the kitchen which was filled with modern appliances and marbled

worktops. 'How did you manage to cook this so quickly?' he asked.
'I used the microwave, of course,' she replied. 'Watch the plate. It's a little hot.'
He had heard of microwave technology, but it wasn't universally available for mass domestic use until the eighties. He tentatively tried a little of the chicken. It was a revelation. His mother had been a very competent cook, but had never been very adventurous with her dishes and had used few herbs in her safe but tasty efforts.
'It seems I do like an Indian meal,' he said between mouthfuls. 'This is delicious – beats hospital food any day.'
'It's about time we went out to a proper Indian restaurant,' she said. 'If you like this, you'll absolutely adore a real Indian meal. These are mass produced, but they're good for a quick meal at home. We don't eat out often enough. We can afford it every once in a while.'
'What do you do – at work, I mean?' he asked. This was a question he'd wanted to ask for some time but other matters had overtaken his wish.
'I'm a Business Development Manager,' she replied.
'Oh ... does that mean you develop businesses?' he asked.
'No ... it means I develop systems for the business,' she answered.
'What do you mean – the business?'
'For our company – that's what we call it.'
'So why aren't you called a Systems Development Manager?' he asked.
'Because we already have one of those. He manages a team that designs and develops our products.'
'Which are?'

'Office equipment. It's mainly office furniture; work stations and the like. Most office environments these days require their employees to work on a computer, so the furniture has to incorporate all the network connections and safe electrical sockets so that you don't have wires trailing all over the place. Many companies like their office to have a sort of corporate image, so we do a lot of bespoke tailoring to their requirements.'

'I have a plain old wooden desk at our place,' he said. '... or at least I did, but then I was the youngest in our office. What are these systems which you develop?'

'Well, the one we're working on at the moment allows the employees a portal to enter their own absence and holiday requests. Their managers then receive an e-mail to say that they need to authorise it through their own portal which of course looks a little different to the employee's. This is all feeds into HR's database which records everything.'

'What's this portal?' he asked. 'Is it like a clocking machine?'

'No, it's part of our intranet. As I said, everyone has a computer on their desk these days. It's all client/server based. It's hard to explain. When we get a few minutes, I'll demonstrate some things on our computer.'

'We have a computer?' he said.

'Everyone has a computer – well nearly everyone. It's become virtually indispensable nowadays. In fact, if we suddenly lost the internet, the world would grind to a halt, but we can discuss that tomorrow, not tonight. I'm working from home for the next few days until I'm happy you can manage on your own. And I need to try to awaken your memories. We'll start with a wander around the garden and the scene of your accident. I'll open a bottle of beer for us to share. We can drink it on the patio.'

After the meal, they went outside. Rob was deeply impressed to discover that they had a patio with a table and some chairs and up one corner, a large barbecue. Julie placed the two beers on the table and led him a little way down the garden path. She said 'That's the tree where you banged your head. You slipped on that root, lost your balance and hit the branch which of course has been there for years, and you knew of its presence, but still you contrived to hit it. Then you fell back and hit the back of your head on the rockery. You had us all very worried when we saw the blood and you weren't moving. Surely, you must remember some of that?'
'The only thing I remember is waking up in the hospital bed. I'm sorry. I am trying.'
'I know you are, love,' she said and squeezed his hand. That simple act made him feel something akin to affection for her.
'This is a lovely garden,' he said. 'I love that seat in the corner.'
'The arbour seat? You made that,' she said.
'What? I made that. I couldn't have made that. I ducked out of woodwork at school because I was cack-handed.'
'Well, I can assure you that you made it. You followed some instructions from a book, but you made it. I helped sometimes just to hold it in place for you, but you made it. And you made that composter at the end of the garden.'
'I don't believe this,' he said. 'I sometimes think I've woken up as a completely different person. Apart from all this carpentry, it seems I'm now an expert on cryptic crosswords when I've never been interested. You told me that I was too tight to buy a decent 'phone when I've always been guilty of squandering my money. I now like spicy food and apparently, I get upset about politics.'

'Oh Rob, everybody gets upset about politics as they get older. You didn't used to be interested – nor did I – but that's an age thing. As for crosswords, when you were working in Lynn, you had a colleague who introduced you to crosswords in your lunch breaks.'
Rob seemed to accept this and she continued. 'When we first got married, you were a right bodger when it came to DIY jobs, but over time, you've worked out your limitations and by taking your time, you've steadily improved. You won't tackle electrics or plumbing, for which I'm quite grateful; and as for being tight, you're not. You always pay your way when it comes to buying a round of drinks or something like that, but what you have to bear in mind is that when we first got married, things were very tight and we had to make sacrifices in order to buy our own house and furnish it. We hardly had a holiday in our first few years. There is a difference between being mean and taking care to manage your finances. Then just as we were making progress, you lost your job and we went through another dodgy period, but we've come through it all and I think we can say we now live comfortably. I bring home a decent salary nowadays. Now stop worrying about silly things.'
'If you say so,' he said, 'but sometimes I think I'm on some kind of acid trip. Everything is weird. Cars open their doors on their own; computers now rule the world; people walk around in a daze staring at these magical mobile phones which can take pictures; girls wear scruffy jeans instead of trying to look smart – and yet we don't have a moon-base or a colony on Mars, fifty years after landing on the moon.
'You know I had an acid trip once,' he added.
'Yes, you told me. It was before we met. You were still in your teens weren't you?'

'Yes, I was talked into it by an older colleague on a night out. I'd had too much to drink and he took me to a party where there were lots of people doing it. I wouldn't have even been there if he hadn't already plied me with so much drink. It was like an horrendous nightmare. I saw all sorts of horrible images in my mind, none of which made any sense. I've never understood why anyone would want to indulge. Have you ever tried it?'
'No, you know I haven't,' she said, forgetting that he didn't know.
They had reached the bottom of the garden and he gazed around at the surroundings. There were attractive cottages on each side and some kind of paddock over their back fence. It was so peaceful and he said so.
'Yes, it's a nice village,' she said. 'There are two pubs and a church. You do sometimes hear the traffic going past on the main road and when the wind's in a certain direction, you can hear the trains, particularly the heavy freight.'
They turned back towards the house and Rob was able to take in the view of the rear of the house. That was when he noticed the satellite dish under the back bedroom. 'Is that a satellite dish?' he asked.
'Yes,' she replied.
'Do we have a radio telescope or something?'
She laughed. 'Oh, that is so silly. No, that's for the television.'
He felt silly, but was it as silly as expecting television to be received via a dish? After all, he had spotted a conventional aerial attached to their chimney stack.
She saw the crestfallen look on his face and realised how that must have sounded. He had always been a little too sensitive. 'Oh, come inside and I'll demonstrate how it works.'

Rob wasn't sure if he was looking forward to retiring for the night. He certainly felt tired enough despite spending much of the last few days in bed. His concern was that he would be sleeping with a woman in her late fifties and he was unsure of his duty. He had previously checked out the bedrooms when he had gone upstairs for his shave and found that there was only one bed made up. There had never been a problem becoming aroused with Kate, but she had been a desirable young woman. Julie was surely very attractive for her age, but she wasn't Kate, and he felt it was a little disloyal to Kate's memory to even consider any sexual activity with this other woman.
'You use the bathroom first,' Julie said. 'You take less time than me.'
He did as he was told, but he had a small dilemma. 'Which is my toothbrush?' he called out not recognising either of the two brushes as conventional implements.
'The one with a blue band,' she replied.
He picked it up and applied the paste. The ridiculously small head meant it was going to take a while to complete the task. Julie had followed him into the bathroom a minute later and laughed at his effort. 'You have to turn it on, silly,' she said, once again using the word *silly* to describe him. 'There is a button in the middle of the stem,' she added.
How was he to know a toothbrush needed turning on?
While Julie then took her turn in the bathroom, he determined to change as quickly as possible and found his pyjamas under one of the pillows. He realised that this must be his side of the bed as the other pillow hid a female garment of some type. 'Do I have any pyjama bottoms?' he called out.

'You don't normally wear them,' she replied. 'I'll find some if you want them.'
'It's all right,' he said and quickly got into bed so as to avoid the embarrassment of changing in front of her. As he wasn't wearing trousers, he decided for the sake of decency to leave his underpants on. He laid his spectacles on the bedside table, let his head drop down on the pillow and closed his eyes, hoping that this would be the end of their interaction for the night. It had only just started to darken outside. A few days ago, it had been late September, but now weirdly it was June.
When Julie entered the bedroom, she turned on the light. Realising that his eyes had been closed, she said 'Sorry. You weren't asleep already were you?'
'No ... no ... I am a little tired, though.'
'Aren't you going to help me undress? You usually do.'
How was he going to react to that request? He wasn't sure that he wanted to even go to bed with someone of her age let alone help her undress. After all, she had been managing perfectly well without him for a few days.
'I think it's important for you to behave as much as usual,' she said. 'It may help your memory. I want you to familiarise yourself with the familiar' She was pleased with her new expression which summed up her thoughts. She removed her trousers exposing her legs.
'What do you think?' she asked. 'Are they still in good condition?'
He realised that he was cornered and reached for his spectacles. He was expecting to see a pair of legs affected by nearly sixty years of wear and tear, with cellulite, wrinkles or unsightly veins. There were none of these things. Her thighs were smooth, firm and very shapely. They could have belonged to someone very much younger. She transferred her weight from one leg

to the other to accentuate the impressive definition. 'Well?' she asked impatiently.
'They are wonderful,' he said feeling like some kind of creepy pervert, but unable to remove his gaze.
'Well, you're partly responsible for that,' she said.
'Me? How?'
'You put me on a training regime. Your favourite word is *metabolics.* According to you, it's all about metabolics. Are you going to crack your favourite joke?'
'I would if I knew it,' he said.
'You usually say *metal what?'*
He laughed. 'That's very funny,' he said.
'Well, it's your joke. Do you know, that's the first time I've heard you laugh since your accident? Welcome back.'
She proceeded to remove her blouse and draped it across a chair, turning to reveal a black bra that matched her panties. It was struggling to contain her ample breasts but Rob's gaze was directed to her panties. Who would have thought that a woman in her late fifties would wear such a skimpy garment? She brazenly turned to allow him to view her gorgeous bottom.
In comparison, Kate's derriere had been small and pert. At that time, he had felt that to be the ideal shape and indeed, for someone of Kate's petite build, it was, but Julie was a different proposition entirely. Although her buttocks were so much larger than Kate's, they were totally in keeping with the rest of Julie's impressive physique. There might have been a slight hint of cellulite, but they were perfectly round and firm and again, by shifting her weight from one leg to the other, she was able to change their shape to demonstrate their beauty.
Rob was pleased that he had continued to wear his underpants because he could feel them straining to

contain his erection. At least he now knew that that part of his anatomy was still working, although the after effects of the catheter caused a little discomfort.
He wasn't sure what he should be doing. She had asked him to help her undress, but so far, she had managed perfectly well without his assistance and he was still sitting in bed nervously watching, knowing that she was in control of this situation.
She tantalisingly pushed her buttocks towards him and with a wiggle, sat down with her back in his direction. 'Are you going to undo my bra?' she said. 'You like doing that.'
He felt that he had never undone a bra in his life. In fact, his sexual experience was distinctly lacking for a twenty year old, which had been mostly with Kate in the back of his car. He had managed penetration a few times, but fear of an unwanted pregnancy had led to the frustration of incompletion of the act. Encounters with a previous girlfriend had been no more successful and now he was nervous.
His hands were shaking as he fumbled with the clasps holding her bra in position. This wasn't helped by the sight of her delicious back and shoulders which were broad and sturdy. Her skin was almost flawless save for two small brown spots and a skin tag. To him, it was inconceivable that a person could be excited by the sight of a woman's back, but he was. He wanted to run his fingers across her skin, but he was unsure if this would be acceptable even though this was his wife and she had thrust her beautiful back in his direction. The last clasp was proving more stubborn than the rest. He supposed that this was because it was now solely supporting the weight of her magnificent breasts, but at last it was free.
'You can touch me if you like,' she said as though it was the obvious thing to do and he ran his hands over

her shoulders and down across her shoulder blades. All the time, his member was straining in his underpants. He then moved his hands up to her sturdy neck and back down her arms which were well toned.
She stood up and turned. After briefly holding her bra in place, she removed it and dropped it on top of her other things on the chair. Rob continued to stare at her breasts. He had expected them to droop down to her stomach, but they only fell a short distance. He couldn't help but notice a little flesh around her midriff which was only to be expected for someone in her fifties and for someone who had given birth to two children.
'I see you're showing signs of recovery,' she said staring at his underwear.
'I'm sorry,' he said for some strange reason.
'Well, I hope you don't think you're getting into my bed in that condition,' she said sternly as though he were a naughty boy. 'No, you can take those pants off for a start ... and those pyjamas.' Then she had a thought. 'The doctors said you can't drive a car. Did they say anything about other things you mustn't do?'
'Er, no,' he said, still unsure of himself.
'That's all right, then. Get those things off!'
'You know I'm not very experienced don't you?' he said.
She laughed. 'This is the Casanova who stole my virginity away from me. Not very experienced! What a load of old rubbish! Now get those things off and lay back. I'll show you experience!'
He did as he was told. She removed her panties and lay down next to him. 'Oh, I love this chest,' she said, 'It's so masculine,' and she kissed it and started to breathe heavily. Her hand found his member and she stroked it expertly.
After a minute of bliss, he found her climbing on top of him and smothering him with her breasts. 'Bring back any memories, yet?' she asked.

'I can safely say that I don't remember ever doing this,' he said. 'But I'm hoping for more. I wasn't sure if people of our age still indulge in sexual activity.'
'Oh, yes,' she said. 'We do it every birthday – well, probably not every birthday, but guess what? Today's my birthday!'
'Is it really? You should have said.'
'Of course it's not my birthday.' With that she skilfully inserted his still erect member within her. It was the most incredible sensation he had ever known. Entering Kate had never felt like this, but then he wasn't always sure if Kate was fully turned on during their encounters in the back of his motor.
Her movement was slow and rhythmical. She had obviously performed this motion many times before. He dearly hoped only with him. He tried to respond by arching his back and reciprocating the movement but his spine was stiffer than he expected it to be and she said 'Just lay still. This works for both of us.'
A thought suddenly struck him. 'Do we need to take precautions?' he asked.
She laughed which caused her to interrupt her motion momentarily. 'You had a vasectomy twenty years ago ... and the only eggs I'm going to produce these days are when I visit the supermarket!'
She continued with her slow piston like action and Rob decided he needed to do something with his hands. At first, he directed them to her back, then her shoulders and along her arms. For the first time, he reached for her breasts which felt so round and full. After a minute, he moved on to her hips, deciding that it was gallant to bypass her tummy with its extra flesh. At last, he reached her buttocks and he grasped them firmly, pulling himself into her as hard as he could. They were magnificent. She was magnificent. At that point, he decided that perhaps he should take over more of the

work and attempted to roll her over, but she was having none of it. He might have managed to roll her with a giant effort, but he could tell she didn't want him to and so he relaxed and continued to enjoy it, but was he enjoying it too much? He wanted this to last forever and he was reaching the point of no return. He'd heard that thinking of something else can extend the act, but all he could think of was Kate and how different it would be with her.
Julie was bringing him to a climax and because he wanted to be sure she would join him, he said 'I'm going to come.' This merely spurred her on and at last, he exploded in a pulsating orgasm that exceeded anything he'd ever know. Julie tried to continue, but it was soon clear that he had subsided and gravity was causing his member to slip away.
She ceased and remained on top of him for a while and he now found it uncomfortable, but didn't dare say so. His hands were now back at his sides.
She kissed him on the lips and rolled off, panting.
'I'm sorry,' he said. 'I wanted you to come as well. I tried to stop you.'
'I didn't want to stop,' she said, 'but now you can finish me off. You're very good at that.'
He was and he knew he was because he perfected the act with Kate. His first girlfriend who was more experienced had taught him how. She had told him to find 'the little man in a boat.' Kate's had been harder to find, but he had managed. Now Julie felt different again. Were all women built differently, he wondered, but she was soon making appreciative noises.
At the end, he just wanted to lay back and fall asleep, but Julie leaned over and kissed him passionately which felt wonderful. 'I do love you,' she said.

‘You’re wonderful,’ he said. He wasn’t sure whether that was a suitable response to a statement of love, but he was sure that he could love her in time.

Chapter 8

Rob woke up feeling a little cold. It had been a warm night up until then and he had not felt the need to retrieve his garments after his earlier vigorous activity, but the temperature had dropped during the early hours of the morning. The sun was not yet up but the pale sky indicated that dawn was not too far away and just enough light filtered through the window for him to see where he had hurled his pyjamas onto the floor. He crept out of bed to fetch them but couldn't see his underpants which were a darker colour so they would have to wait.

Julie was still naked and he wondered if he should find her nightwear, but that might involve waking her, so he considerately decided against it.

He felt that their earlier intimacy had at last broken down an invisible barrier of his own making. He still held deep feelings for Kate, but he had to put them to one side as he rebuilt his relationship with his wonderful wife.

As he lay there, he still had a hundred questions he needed answering. If he couldn't get back to sleep, he would use the time to prioritise these. The most important question on his mind was probably in regards to his career. He knew nothing about being a personal trainer and didn't know whether Julie would be able to help him get back to work. He assumed that he possessed some kind of qualification for his job but that would be of no use if he didn't know how to perform it. Julie had mentioned something about him helping her with a training regime. Did that mean he was her personal trainer? That could be interesting, he thought.

Before he could think of any more questions that needed answering, he fell deeply into sleep and a world of dreams. An hour later he was woken by the sound of

the dawn chorus and movement from his wife. *His wife!* He was still getting used to the notion that he had a wife and that he was in bed with her.
'Noisy birds,' she said stretching her arms. 'Why don't they have a lie-in for once?'
'I love it,' Rob said with his own stretch. 'I've never heard their song as loud as this before. I could do without the magpies though.'
'Yes, you've always hated the magpies. They eat other birds' eggs and their young.'
'They do?' he asked.
'Well, you told me,' she said.
'I did? I must be a clever person to know all that,' he said.
'You get a lot of your knowledge from *QI*,' she said.
'What's that?' he asked.
'A television programme,' she replied.
'Is that the one with Spike Milligan?'
'No, it's Steven Fry,' she replied. 'Or rather it was. It's now chaired by Sandi Toksvig. You've probably never heard of her either. It will become clearer when you watch some of the old episodes. They're always being repeated on Dave. That's a TV channel.'
'A channel called Dave? Is there one called Fred, as well?'
She smiled at that.
Did you have a good sleep?' he asked
'I did, thank you – and you?' she responded.
'Yes. This is a comfortable bed, but I did wake up once just before dawn. I was feeling a little cold and needed my pyjamas. I was going to get your nightdress, but I would have disturbed you and you sounded so peaceful.'
'Was I snoring again?' she asked.
'No, just breathing deeply,' he replied. 'Has our sex life always been as wonderful as it was last night?'

'We've always managed. When we first got married, it was more a case of quantity than quality. We were like two rabbits doing it as often as we could. There was a lot of experimenting – different positions – you on top; me on top; standing up; sitting down; bondage; leather; dressing up; the flying helmet with the celery.'
'What? Where does celery come in?' he asked, not sure if he believed any of it.
'You'll have to watch *'Allo 'Allo,'* she said. 'It's a comedy programme, made in the eighties I would think. It's about the French Resistance. The programme made fun of everyone – the French, the English, the Germans, the Gestapo, the Communist Resistance; just about everyone. They're still showing regular repeats. It wouldn't get made these days. But as I say, at least you can see the repeats; unlike *It Ain't Half Hot Mum,* which never gets aired.
'I like that,' said Rob. 'What's wrong with it?'
'I think it was seen as degrading to the Indian characters and the sergeant chap was always calling the gang a load of poofs. Then they had a white man blacking up to play an Indian. That still upsets some people.'
'Oh, dear: How sad. Never mind,' said Rob quoting one of the catchphrases from the show. 'So there's no chance of seeing *The Black and White Minstrels* then?'
He was joking of course, but Julie said 'Now that was silly. All those men blacking up like that. I couldn't see the point.'
'Neither could I,' said Rob, 'but my father used to like it. It was the singing that he enjoyed. Was it the George Mitchell singers? There was a joke about George Mitchell. What's the difference between a young child and George Mitchell?'
'I don't know,' she replied.

'One sucks its fingers ...' He paused for the laughter that never came. 'I'm not sure if he was that way inclined but that didn't stop people making a joke about it.'
'If it had been so, we'd have heard about it by now,' Julie said. 'There would have been *historical allegations*. In any case, they wouldn't get away with a show like that today. Everything's too PC.'
'What's PC?'
'Oh dear, my love. You have so much to catch up on. We must get your memory back to normal. Perhaps you could spend the day watching some old television and listening to some of your old music. That ought to awaken something. I have to get on with some work. I've lost quite a bit of time this week – and you need to 'phone the surgery to get an appointment to get your dressing changed. When was it last changed?'
'Yesterday morning,' he replied. 'Is it Thursday today?' The days of the week didn't mean a lot to him at that moment.
'Yes, it is,' she replied. 'I don't know if it's worth getting it changed tomorrow and I doubt if you will get an appointment over the weekend. It will have to be Monday – if they can fit you in that is. I'll have to drive you there, which means more time lost – and then there's your next appointment at the hospital. Perhaps after that, you can start driving again.'
She leaned over and kissed him on the forehead, carefully avoiding his bandage. 'I'd better get up,' she said and did so revealing her wonderful bottom to him. He reached for his spectacles before she donned a dressing gown. He could feel his member stirring again. Even though this was his wife, he felt embarrassed about his ardour and he decided to stay in bed until it subsided, especially as he still wasn't wearing any underpants.

As Julie headed for the bathroom, she caught sight of his underwear where it had been thrown to the floor. 'I'll put these in the washing basket,' she said, handling them as though she might catch something. 'It's about time you wore some clean ones. They're in that drawer with your clean socks. Your shirts are in the wardrobe. I'm going to have a shower.'

While Julie finished her shower, Rob went down to explore the kitchen. He knew that this was his house but he felt like an intruder and was reluctant to help himself to breakfast without first obtaining Julie's approval. After all, he knew that he was taking tablets for high blood pressure so perhaps he had to watch what he ate as well.

However, that didn't prevent him from opening various cupboards to discover their contents. Many of the food items that he found were alien to him. Even the breakfast cereals were unfamiliar. The contents of one packet looked like birdseed. Others were mixed with unappetising dried fruit. What happened to good old Corn Flakes and Rice Krispies?

He thought that perhaps the large refrigerator might be more promising. It seemed that milk no longer came in glass bottles. One plastic container was described as semi-skimmed. He hoped that was for Julie. He liked his cereal milk to contain a layer of cream on the top. Other than that, there were no great surprises except that this appliance was much larger than his parents, particularly the freezer section with its three separate drawers. His parents' freezer section was barely large enough for one tray of ice cubes and a packet of fish fingers; or possibly fish cakes, but not both.

He noticed that the work surfaces of the kitchen were surprisingly clear of clutter. The plates and beer

glasses from their evening meal had been removed. He didn't recall Julie washing those, so had she perhaps come down during the night to do it? He hadn't spotted the dishwasher. The house itself was also free of clutter. That was quite an achievement considering that Julie held down a full time job.
When she did arrive, she was able to tell him that he could eat anything he wanted but pointed him to his current favourite cereal and told him to add some raspberries for added flavour.
As he sat down to eat, he asked 'I was wondering about my job. Should I be doing anything about it?'
'It's all right for now,' she replied. 'I've cancelled all your appointments for the next couple of weeks. It's lucky that you keep an old-fashioned diary to keep track of them. Most people would have used a computer or their 'phone, but you have it all written down with times, addresses and contact details. You've probably also got their telephone numbers on your 'phone, but this way, if you lose a signal or the battery's flat, you won't have a problem.'
'Do I have a place of work?' he asked.
'You go to several places. The main one is a local gym, but you sometimes hold a class in a village hall and you even visit one or two people in their homes. One lady has an expensive multi-gym that her husband bought her for a present before realising that she didn't know how to use it.'
'That all sounds quite interesting,' he said, 'except that I don't know how to use one myself. If I've already taught her how to use the equipment, does she still need me?'
'You told me that if you're not there, she is afraid to use it on her own – and you motivate and encourage her. You do that for a lot of your clients who would probably give up without you to bully them.'

‘I can’t imagine me being a bully,’ he said. ‘Am I your personal trainer as well?’
‘Oh, no, no, no – no way. We tried it for a while, but it’s like teaching your wife to drive. It’s not a good idea if you want to stay together, but you did get me started. Now I prefer to do my own thing when I workout. I’m not one to need pushing. You taught me how to avoid injury which is something a lot of beginners get wrong. For other people, you find out what they want to achieve and help with diets. So many people, who want to lose weight, make the mistake of just cutting down on food, but that doesn’t always work. Your big message is all about metabolics.’
‘Metal what?’ he asked.
‘...bolics,’ she said, pleased that he had remembered his joke.
‘I only asked,’ he said and she smiled. It was almost as though the old Rob was back.
‘Are all my clients female?’ he asked.
‘No, you have a bit of a mix, but you find that a lot of the men are happy to go off and do their own thing a lot sooner than the ladies. Or perhaps, the females all succumb to your charm like I did all those years ago. Perhaps I should be feeling jealous.’
‘I don’t think so – not if last night was anything to go by,’ he said with a lecherous grin on his face.
‘Typical man! Only thinks of one thing!’

‘Thank you for calling the Uppingham Surgery,’ said a recorded voice on the telephone. ‘All our operators are busy at the moment. Your call will be answered as soon as one is free.’
Rob was about to relay this information to Julie, when a second voice said ‘You are currently number eight in the queue.’

'I'm number eight in a queue,' he said.
'For Heaven's sake,' Julie said. 'They've only just opened up the switchboard. Just keep hanging on for a while.'
'I've just had someone else tell me that I can book an appointment online. What does that mean?' he asked.
Julie had her office laptop in front of her. 'I'll have a look,' she said, 'but I don't know your password so I can't book it.' Rob had no idea what she was doing. 'The earliest appointment with a nurse is Tuesday, Julie said. 'That's nearly a week after your dressing was last changed. That's no good. Just hang on in the queue. You need to talk to someone.'
'I'm now number seven in the queue,' he said.
Eventually, the annoying music and the repetitive messages ceased and a real human being spoke to him. 'Sorry to keep you waiting. How can I help you?'
'Oh, hello. I was discharged from hospital yesterday with a head injury and I was told to contact my GP to have the dressing changed.'
'What's your date of birth?' the voice asked abruptly.
Rob couldn't understand why his date of birth was relevant but he mumbled his reply.
'And your surname? She asked.
'Lennard – that's L-E-, double N, A-R-D,' he replied.
'Paddock View, South Luffenham?'
He suddenly realised that he didn't know his home address, but it sounded right, so he just said 'Yes,' but without conviction.
'I can fit you in this afternoon – at two forty. We've just had a cancellation.'
'Er ... I've only just had a fresh dressing yesterday. I was thinking I need to give it another day or two,' he replied.
'I've got nothing else until Tuesday at three forty,' the operator said.

'That will be almost a week without changing it. I only need a quick five minutes with someone.'
'Wait a minute,' the lady said and the annoying music started again.
'What did she say?' Julie asked.
'She just told me to wait a minute,' he said.
After a few more minutes, the lady said 'Can you get here at eight thirty Monday morning? The nurse can fit you in before her other appointments.'
'I'll have to ask my wife. I can't drive at the moment. Julie, can you take me for eight thirty on Monday?' Julie nodded. 'Yes, we can make that.'
'I'll send you a text,' the lady said. 'So that's Monday the seventeenth at eight thirty.'
Rob had no idea what a text message was but he was very relieved to put down the 'phone. Does having high blood pressure cause this unease or was it just these modern automated answering services and their annoying music?
After he had composed himself, he asked Julie how she had looked up the appointments.
'I need to get on with some work just now,' she said,' but I will show you later. We probably need to check your own messages at some point, but for now, just amuse yourself with the television or the newspapers. You probably still need to take things easy. Now, I need to 'phone one of my team leaders to update him on yesterday's meeting and update the documentation, so close the door behind you.'
Rob obeyed her but felt belittled both by her domination and her priorities and didn't want to take things easy. He had been lying about for several days and he wanted to find out more about himself and this 'Brave New World' into which he had been thrust. To satisfy the latter curiosity, he picked up the latest newspaper.

There was more about this 'Brexit' business and politicians he had never heard of. He noticed that many of the Royal family were new to him, too. Prince Charles still seemed to be next in line to the throne, but he had married the Duchess of Cornwall. Rob didn't realise that there was a Duchess of Cornwall, but perhaps he had married her to cement an alliance with Cornwall as princes once did in olden days. His guess was that the Cornish had been demanding independence and this was a way of appeasing them.
He tried once more to work on a cryptic crossword, but he still struggled and even the General Knowledge crosswords required a more up-to-date appreciation of facts than he possessed.
Just before they had retired the night before, Julie had briefly demonstrated the television, but there were so many buttons on so many remote controls that now that he tried it for himself, he was left floundering. The television listings showed that there were hundreds of programmes he could be watching, but there were so many codes to key in to get the various channels that he was even more confused. There were satellite codes, Freeview codes, Freesat codes, HD codes and +1, whatever that was. There were even codes for 'Virgin!' In Rob's day, there were just four channels and one of them wasn't available in his area. He kept pressing buttons until he hit on a weird programme about renovating a house. So many channels; was this the best he could find? After ten minutes, he turned it off and just sat there, trying to relax and taking in his new surroundings.
Eventually, Julie re-appeared and said 'I'm sorry to have abandoned you like that, but I had to get that bit of work out of the way. Shall we have a coffee? And then we need to put the dishwasher on.'

Rob wondered about his wife. One minute she was fierce and domineering, the next she was sweetness and light. Kate was always sweetness and light, but he had never lived with her, so perhaps this was what marriage was all about.
'I've been thinking,' said Julie. 'If you were to see Barney and Belinda, that might trigger off some kind of memory. How would you like that?'
Rob was certainly keen to see their mother Sarah again. He thought she was lovely, both to look at and to be with, so he was happy to see all of them. 'What did you have in mind?' he asked.
'Well, I like to go to the gym after work on a Thursday. It would be nice if we could go together, but it would be awkward if any of your clients were there after cancelling all your appointments and I don't know if I should leave you on your own so early after leaving hospital. Sarah's house is almost on the way, so I could drop you off with them and pick you up on the way back – and I'll pick up a Chinese take away from Stamford to bring back. We had an Indian last night so we don't want that again. You like a Chinese.'
'Do they do spare ribs?' he asked. 'They do marvellous spare ribs at that place on the corner in Gaywood – or they did.'
'You remember them?' she said.
'Yes, we often had them after a night out,' he said. 'We would eat them in the car and make a mess.'
'That's wonderful! You remember us having those. That's a start.'
'Er, no. I don't remember having them with you. It was with someone else ... sorry.'
That memory stirred up his feelings for Kate and he had to fight off the emotion. 'Yes, let's do that,' he added, realising that he had to think exclusively of his new wife.

Julie sighed and then said ‘That’s what we’ll do then – assuming Sarah’s all right with it. I’ll give her a call in a minute. Now what sort of coffee do you want?’
Rob thought that was a strange question for a wife to ask. ‘White with sugar,’ he replied.
‘I know that,’ she said, ‘but do you want latte, cappuccino, Americano, or what?’
‘I don’t know what they are,’ he said. ‘I just want an ordinary coffee.’ He assumed they would have a cup of instant coffee from a jar.
‘We have a machine,’ she said. ‘I’ll just do you an Americano for now. You see, you just feed in one of these pods, check the water level and press a button and make sure there’s a cup underneath of course or it makes a mess. While we’re drinking the coffee, I’ll show you what the internet is all about, then you can amuse yourself with it while I get on with some more work.’

Chapter 9

Almost on the dot of five o'clock, Julie closed her laptop for the day and informed Rob that she was going to get changed ready for her visit to the gym. He finished looking at a web site where he would be able to purchase all manner of wonderful items that he never knew he needed. Julie had told him not to buy anything without her checking that he didn't already possess that item or something similar. In any case, he would need to have a user ID, password or some other piece of information outside of his current knowledge for that to be possible and she wasn't prepared to divulge such information at that time.

She had pointed him to some safer web sites such as those that would supply the news, sport or weather, just to get him familiar with the concept of the internet, but joked that he would have to find his favourite porn sites himself.

'Do people pawn stuff online?' he asked innocently.

'Not that sort of pawn, dear. I meant porn ... as in your old porn magazines that you used to hide. Everything's on-line, these days.'

Rob had never understood the need for porn magazines, even when he was unattached and he stared at her with open eyes.

'I'm joking,' she said. 'I don't think you've ever been interested in porn magazines, but I can't know everything, can I?' She had a mischievous glint in her eye.

For the rest of his time on the internet, he made a few notes of things that he might want to revisit at a later date, but they didn't include porn.

When Julie re-appeared, she was wearing a blue sleeveless top and black leggings that revealed the shape of her wonderful legs and bottom. Perhaps standards had changed in the last forty years, but Rob wasn't sure that he approved of her going out in public in that state, while at the same time enjoying the view for himself. He was looking forward to bedtime that night. In fact, he'd been looking forward to it all day and her current appearance wasn't going to help.

'Did you have fun on the internet?' she asked as they drove along.
'It was fascinating,' he replied. 'I would think that it has really changed the world.'
'It has,' she said. 'For one thing, you can buy almost anything on the internet – and it's usually cheaper than in the shops. All the big stores have their own web sites. They have to in order to compete – M&S, Currys, John Lewis; all the supermarkets and the DIY stores.'
'What about C & A? That's one of my favourite places for clothes,' he said.
'No, they closed down years ago.'
'Woolworths?'
'No, they're closed,'
'Woolworths closed? It can't be. What about Foster Menswear?'
'No.'
'That's some of my favourite shops,' he said. 'I hope there are some good ones to take their place.'
'You get a lot of your clothes from charity shops,' Julie said half in jest. 'There are loads of them in every town. There's not much choice for men in Stamford. By the way, I meant to tell you ... we're babysitting Saturday night, so it's as well you're seeing Barney and Belinda today.'

The journey to Ketton did not take long and Sarah was waiting at the door so Julie dropped off Rob and headed off to her gym.
'Hello Dad,' Sarah said, giving him a warm embrace. 'How are you today?'
He realised that he enjoyed the embrace much more than he should have done, but he still struggled to believe that this gorgeous young woman was his daughter. 'I'm fine, thank you,' he said, taking a lingering but embarrassed look at her.
'I'm glad you're here,' Sarah said. 'I want to give Belinda a bath, but Neville's not home yet, so I'm hoping you can entertain Barney for a while. He's looking forward to seeing you.'
'Yes, if you think I can be trusted with him. I'm not allowed to stay at home on my own, but I can look after a five year old.' He realised that he sounded a little petulant, but he had been gradually feeling more and more frustrated at his condition, not to say confused with his lack of knowledge about modern technology.
'Oh, Dad! I know it's all frustrating for you, but you just have to be a little patient until you get the all-clear from the doctors. Come and say hello to the children. They always cheer you up.'
Belinda was watching television on a huge screen as Rob entered the sitting room, while Barney was playing with some toy cars. 'Look who's here,' said Sarah. 'It's Grandad!'
Barney spoke first, without looking up, 'There's been a bad accident. The ambulance is coming. These silly people weren't wearing their seat belts.'
Sarah said,' Belinda – say hello to Grandad.'
'Is Nanny here?' the young girl asked without looking away from the television.
'No, but Grandad's here.'

So much for the two children looking forward to seeing him. Rob looked around at the decor in the room. It was not to his taste. The walls were off-white and devoid of any pictures although a large mirror hung above the imitation fireplace. The floor was all polished wood save for a small rug in front of the fireplace. The three-piece suite was grey and matched the curtains. The room did not seem welcoming, but apart from the toys strewn on the floor, it was clean and probably functional.

'Hello Belinda,' Rob said.

'I'm not Belinda. I'm Elsa.'

'She's into *Frozen* at the moment,' Sarah said. 'They're both tired. Come on, Belinda. You need a bath, young lady.'

'I just want to see the end of this programme,' Belinda said, not taking her eyes away from the screen.

'How long has it got to go?' Sarah asked.

'Don't know,' came the reply.

Sarah picked up a remote control and information about the programme was super-imposed on the screen.

'Ten minutes,' said Sarah. 'And then you're off upstairs.'

Rob saw from the screen that the programme she was watching was called *In the Night Garden* and looked silly with unrealistic characters, but then, in his day, *The Clangers* were also quite silly. He turned his attention to Barney. 'Can I play with you?' he asked.

'You can have the ambulance,' Barney said. Rob wasn't sure what he was supposed to do with the ambulance, but at least his presence had been acknowledged.

When Belinda's programme had finished, Sarah turned off the television. 'Ooooh!' said Belinda. 'I don't want a bath.'

'You can take Anna and Elsa in the bath with you,' Sarah said.

'Yeah!' Belinda said excitedly.
'Barney, it's time for you to tidy up your toys – then perhaps Grandad will read you a story.'
Barney had one more car crash and then violently threw his toys into a box. 'There!' he said as though he was fulfilling an unpleasant task against his will. 'Can we play football?' he asked.
'I don't think we should just now. I've still got a big plaster on my head – and I don't think my doctor would like it.'
'Is he scared you might fall asleep again?' Barney asked.
'I think he's probably more worried about me making it bleed again,' Rob said. 'What book shall we read?'
'*Ivor the Engine!*' the little lad cried and went to fetch it from a wooden chest on the floor.
Rob sat on the grey settee and Barney hurled himself onto his lap and nestled against his shoulder. So this is what being a grandad was all about.
Rob remembered *Ivor the Engine* from the television, but had never watched it nor read any of the books. However, he knew that it was set in Wales and decided that he would read it with a Welsh accent.
'Why are you reading it in that funny voice?' Barney asked.
'Because it's set in Wales – it's The Merioneth and Llantisilly Railway Traction Company Limited. That's how they talk in Wales.'
Barney laughed. 'No, they don't,' he said.
'They do. I've been there and that's how they talk.' Actually, Rob had never been to Wales, at least not as far as he knew, but he'd heard enough Welsh accents on television to mimic them and was doing his best to amuse his grandson. He continued with the story and came to a stop mid-sentence. Something about this

seemed familiar. He had done this before. He recognised the story and the pictures. But how?
Just then, Neville came home and Barney rushed to the door to greet him. 'Dad! Grandad's here. We're reading a story.'
'Hello Rob. How are you feeling?' Neville asked.
Rob thought it was strange that his son-in-law should address him by his Christian name. He would never have dreamed of calling Kate's parents by their first names. It would have been Mr Sanderson or Mrs Sanderson, but that was back in 1979.
'I'm not too bad thank you, but my memory still hasn't returned. You must be Neville.' He thought of reaching out to shake hands but stopped himself.
'Where are the girls?' Neville asked, having not been informed of Rob's visit.
'Sarah's upstairs giving Belinda a bath,' Rob replied.
'I'll just go and see if she needs any help,' Neville said. It was clear that he was just as embarrassed as Rob.
Rob finished the story and closed the book with a flourish.
'Again!' said Barney.
'Again?' replied Rob. 'Haven't you got some other books?'
'Again!' said Barney. 'I like Ivor. Do that funny voice again.'
Because Rob was now more familiar with the story, he was able to pace his reading more effectively and even used different voices for the different characters, but again, it struck a chord. Could this really be the start of regaining his memory?
Neville rejoined them. 'Can I get you a coffee or anything, Rob?' he asked.
'Not for me, thank you,' Rob replied.
Barney insisted on a third reading. 'Haven't you got anything else we can read?' Rob asked.

'No, I like this one,' Barney said wriggling about and almost knocking off his Grandad's spectacles.
'The last time, then,' Rob said.
Neville said 'It's a bit dark where you're sitting. Have some light. Alexa, turn on the lamp.'
'Okay,' a female voice said and the lamp next to the settee lit up.
Rob looked around to see this mysterious Alexa, but there was no one else in the room.
'How did you ...?'
Neville smiled. He loved showing off his device and with Rob's loss of memory, he could start all over again. 'That's Alexa. Ask her a question.'
'I don't understand,' Rob said.
'Alexa,' said Neville, 'What's the capital of Peru?'
'The capital of Peru is Lima,' said the voice.
Rob could see that the voice appeared to be coming from a small device on the shelf in the corner of the room and the device, which resembled a thick ice-hockey puck, was glowing blue as it spoke.
'You ask her a question,' Neville said.
'What's the capital of France?' Rob asked.
There was no response.
'You have to start with *Alexa* to wake up the device,' Neville said. 'Try again.'
'Alexa, what's the capital of France?'
'The capital of France is Paris.'
'What's the ... Alexa, where is Timbuktu?'
'Timbuktu is in Mali,' Alexa said.
'I've often wondered where it was,' said Rob, feeling mightily impressed. 'So she can answer general knowledge questions. It's a bit like the computer in *Star Trek.* And she can turn lights on. Can she read a story to young Barney, here?'
'I want you to read a story,' said Barney. 'Come on, Grandad.'

'I'll show you some other things, later,' said Neville and left them to continue with their story.
A few minutes later, Sarah re-appeared with Belinda who was wearing her night attire. 'How are you two chaps getting on?' she asked.
'We're all right,' said Rob. 'We've just read *Ivor the Engine* three times and I think we were just about to go for a fourth time.'
'That old book?' Sarah said. 'Mum gave us that. You used to read it to me and Ben when we were young. You always read it with a Welsh accent and silly voices.'
'Did I?' Rob said. 'As I was reading it, just now, something felt familiar. I wonder if my memory is starting to return.'
'That's wonderful,' said Sarah. 'Have you remembered anything else?'
'No, just that, but it's a start.'
'Can I have a story?' Belinda asked.
'You go and pick one out and I'll read it,' said her mother.
'No, I want Grandad to read it,' the little one demanded.
'Barney,' said Sarah, 'you haven't had a drink. Let's go and get one while Grandad reads to Belinda.'
'No, I want to hear *Ivor* again.'
'We can read it on Saturday when Grandma and I come babysitting,' said Rob.
'Who's Grandma?' asked Barney.
'He meant Nanny, of course,' said Sarah. 'Come on. You can have some milk.'
Belinda had chosen a picture book called *Clip-Clop* which Rob didn't recognise. Belinda plopped herself on his lap which was still warm from Barney's bottom.
Naturally, when he had finished reading the story, she wanted a repeat.

He was saved a third reading by the arrival of his wife, still wearing her revealing leggings.
'Are you all ready, Rob? The takeaway is getting cold. Sorry, children. We can't stop, but we'll see you again on Saturday.'
Just then, Neville re-appeared. 'Hello, Julie. You look fit.'
Rob was annoyed at their son-in-law's personal comments.
'Nanny's got a big bum like mummy,' said Belinda going over to her and patting it.
'We'll see if you have a big bum when you get a bit bigger,' Julie responded. 'Now we must go. Give me a kiss.'
And they were out of the house before Barney could also detain them.
As they got in the car, Rob could smell the meal. The aroma was coming from the back seat. He turned to see a large cool bag. 'Is it in that bag?' he asked.
'Yes. The cool bag will keep it hot until we get home. They had some spare ribs, but I don't think they're cooked in the same way as the old place in Gaywood. There's also some chicken chow mein, beef in black bean sauce and some egg-fried rice. I'm feeling hungry. How were the kids?'
'They're a handful, but they are great. I read *Ivor the Engine* to Barney and I'm sure I remember reading it before. I hope that's a good sign.'
'So do I,' she replied. 'You used to read that to Ben when he was young. Did you use the Welsh accent and the funny voices?'

Chapter 10

Rob and Julie sat outside on the patio drinking a glass of beer. His parents didn't have a patio, so this was a new experience for him, as was eating a Chinese meal off a warmed plate instead of from a carton in his car getting sticky fingers everywhere. Julie was still wearing her gym outfit and was too lazy to bother changing, not realising the effect it was having on her husband who kept stealing glances in her direction like a dirty old man who had never seen a shapely woman in leggings before.

'Shall we do today's crossword?' she asked.

Rob had other things on his mind, but he reluctantly agreed.

'It's another thing we often do together, so it might help your recovery,' she said when she returned with the newspaper and a pen.

Rob tried to join in, but he was still struggling with the concept of a cryptic crossword, but Julie was patient with him and explained each of her answers. One clue was *Fashionable men creating a friendly society.* Rob was thinking a friendly society might be something to do with the Quakers, or possibly the Co-Op, but Julie penned in *fellowship.*

'How did you get that?' he asked.

'Well, whenever you see *fashionable* in a crossword, it tends to mean one of two things. The usual one is *in*, see, and a lot of words start with those two letters, but the other one is *hip.* Compilers often find that useful at the end of a word, such as *sponsorship* or *relationship.* Then it was a question of finding how that could fit in with the rest of the clue. As we already had the letter *F*, it all followed.'

'That's very clever,' he said, being impressed with his clever wife while wishing he could have thought of it.

'You get used to certain things that get utilised a lot; such as *youth leader* or *group leader* if you're looking for a *Y* or a *G.* The more you do these things, the easier it gets. If you see *sailor* in the clue, it can mean several things, such as *salt, AB,* as in *able-bodied* or sometimes even *OS,* as in *ordinary seaman,* and, of course, *tar.'*
She directed him to a couple of the easier clues and let him have a stab on his own and by the time the evening light was fading, he had made a small contribution, with the puzzle ninety per cent completed. He decided that he would study it again the next day and complete it on his own. He was determined that he would impress his wife, just as he would want to do with any female he'd only known a short time. The crucial clue was *I'm great for writing by Scott.* They had the third letter which was *G.* It looked like an anagram of *I'm great* and the letter 'G' seemed to confirm that, but the only word that seemed to fit was *migrate* and that didn't make sense. Rob wanted to use the word but Julie insisted that there had to be an explanation for it. Because *Scott* was spelt with two Ts, it looked like it could be something to do with Walter Scott, but an online search found nothing of relevance.

'I've got to carry on working all day,' Julie said the next morning over breakfast. 'Do you know how you will be spending the day?'
Rob didn't want to mention the crossword. He was going to surprise her when he had finished it; that was assuming that he was successful, but he would keep quiet for now in case he failed. 'No, not really. I'm sure the internet still holds some surprises for me but I don't

think I should do that all day. Do you have any suggestions?'
'Well, the floors haven't been hoovered since before Sarah's visit on Sunday, so you could do that for a start.'
'Hoovering? You want me to do some hoovering?'
'It's one of your normal jobs,' she said. 'I don't think the doctor said anything about not performing household chores.'
Rob had never picked up a vacuum in his life. That was always his mother's job. His father would certainly never have performed the task; nor any other household chore.
Julie saw the look of horror on his face and decided to have some fun at his expense. She remembered a *Two Ronnies* series called *The Worm that Turned* where the world had changed and women had become the dominating force in the country. Men wore dresses and performed all the household chores and an army of women clad in hot pants marched around enforcing law and order
'I hope this memory loss thing isn't just a ploy to get out of your responsibilities,' she said. 'You were around when Margaret Thatcher came to power, weren't you?'
He nodded.
'That was the start of the sexual revolution. Nowadays, it's usually the woman who is the breadwinner and the man does the household chores. I thought we'd established that soon after we married. You do know we have a female Prime Minister again, don't you? Germany is ruled by a woman. The world has changed since the seventies. Women have the upper hand now.'
His face dropped. She was joking wasn't she? Then again, she was in charge of a team of men at work. Perhaps that was the norm. In the seventies, there had been a lot of talk about women's lib and protests about

equality. She was looking at him in the same fierce way that had unnerved him the first few times she had breezed into the hospital.

But she couldn't maintain it. She burst into laughter. 'Look at your face,' she said. 'Where's my camera? You'll be pleased to know that women don't rule the world, but we do have much more equality nowadays. There is legislation to ensure we're paid the same as men for doing the same jobs. There are now some women doing traditional men's jobs like fire fighting and plumbing, but they are the exception. More to the point, you won't find men working in children's nurseries.'

'There was a male nurse at the hospital,' Rob said.

'Yes, but he would be in the minority. You and I agreed some time ago, that because we both work, we would share some of the household chores – and hoovering is one of yours; not that you're very good at it, but you do try. When you were made redundant all those years ago, you were glad to help out for something to do.'

'All right, but you'll have to show me how to do it,' he said.

'Yeah, it's ever so difficult,' she said with just the slightest hint of sarcasm. 'Anyway, the hoovering won't take that long. What else are you going to do?'

'I have a feeling that you have some ideas about that,' he replied, fearing more household tasks.

'I still want you to regain your memory,' she said. 'So ... I thought you could browse through your CD collection and play one or two of them. They say music evokes memories, don't they?'

'What's a CD?' he asked.

'Really?' She sighed. 'You don't know what a CD is? I thought they'd been around for ages. They're already considered by many to be obsolete. CD stands for compact disc. They're smaller and more durable than your old vinyl. The recordings are made digitally so you won't hear that old scratchy noise you used to get with your old records. Have a look in the cabinet in the sitting room and see what you think. Of course, you may not recognise a lot of them. I'll show you how to operate the CD player ... once you've done the hoovering!'

Hoovering gave him to time to think. That clue in the crossword - *I'm great for writing by Scott.* It had to be an anagram, but which words formed the anagram? They had the third letter which was *G*, so that letter must be part of the anagram. He had it! He felt really pleased with himself.

As they readied to sit down for the morning coffee, he fetched the newspaper with the incomplete crossword and looked at it. 'Ragtime!' he announced.

'What?' she said.

'Ragtime! *I'm great for writing by Scott* it said ... an anagram of *I'm great ... ragtime!'* The *Scott* is Scott Joplin not Walter Scott. He wrote *The Entertainer* which was used in *The Sting.* That's my favourite film, you know.

'I know it is. We've seen it several times,' she said. 'Well done, and now that leaves just one clue,' which she completed having found an extra letter from *ragtime.*

'That's quite rewarding,' he said, '... to complete a crossword together, I mean.'

'Yes,' she said. 'We usually manage to finish them when we work together' and she gave him a kiss on the forehead.

He had to kneel down to the CD cabinet which caused his joints to creek and he found his eyes could not

focus on the writing on the spines of the CDs when looking down at an angle. He'd noticed that since waking from his coma, his eyesight had deteriorated despite wearing corrective glasses. He took out a handful of the cases from the cupboard to make it easier to read. As Julie had suggested, he didn't recognise all of the names, but there were some CDs by Nancy Wilson. He vaguely knew of her from her records in the sixties, such as *How Glad I Am* and *Guess Who I saw Today*. This was the sort of music that his parents might have enjoyed. He guessed that this must be Julie's taste and he continued looking for something familiar from his own choice.
In 1979, disco music was still hanging on and Rob loved a good dance beat, but there was nothing of that ilk so far. Many of the discs seemed to veer towards jazz or middle of the road material; not a disco beat in sight. He had heard a few things by the Crusaders which he felt were all right, but still not the sort of music that he would buy. He carried on looking. The discs were arranged in alphabetical order and at the bottom were several that seemed to cover *Various Artists*. During the seventies, K-Tel had released several LPs where they gathered hits from various artists and conducted a successful television advertising campaign. This was ground-breaking at the time, especially as the artists were usually garnered from different labels. The Various Artists CDs which he was now perusing seemed to cover a wide spectrum. There was a Philadelphia International selection which pleased him as it included lots of familiar disco tracks, so perhaps these were his purchases. He went into the next room to talk to Julie.
'I'm guessing that a lot of these are your ...'
She waved him away.
He tried again. 'I just wanted to ask ...'

'I'm on the 'phone!' she said firmly and gave him a look of annoyance.
Rob had not noticed because her mobile was to the ear away from him and he wasn't used to seeing such small devices held to one's ear. He sloped off back to the CDs feeling both silly and annoyed at the same time. How dare she speak to him like that?
After a few minutes, Julie joined him. 'I'm sorry about that,' she said. 'I was on the 'phone to the HR Manager. She always manages to put me in a bad mood. She only got the job because one of the directors is tupping her.'
'Tupping?' Rob asked. He could guess what it meant, but he still hadn't heard the word before.
'Yes, tupping. A sheep farmer needs a ram to tup his flock.'
'Oh, a ram. I remember being out with my mother once when we saw a ram doing his job and I asked what he was doing. She told me that he needs to go up to each of the lady sheep and say *I love ewe* – see E.W.E – ewe.'
'Very funny,' Julie said. 'Now, what were you saying?'
'It doesn't matter,' he said petulantly as he continued to look at the CDs.
'Oh, come on, love. I said I was sorry.' She knelt down beside him and leant her head on his shoulder.
'I was just asking about these CDs,' he said. 'They don't look like the sort of thing I would buy. I was wondering if some of these are yours.'
'Mine? I've never bought a CD in my life. That's your domain, my love. They're all yours.'
He was puzzled. 'But these aren't the sort of things I buy. Nancy Wilson? The Crusaders?'
'I think you'll find your taste has broadened a little over the years,' she replied. 'When I first met you, you were dead keen on dance music – disco and the like, but

then as disco died out, you and others switched to Jazz-Funk; and then Jazz-Funk mellowed and the Jazz part became more melodic. The clubs mostly turned to electro which we both hated. Synthesisers took over from real instruments. You still like the old stuff, but now you like these other things as well; especially if we sit down together to listen. We often put on an Earl Klugh or Grover Washington album if we're doing the crossword together.'
'What about my old LPs?' he asked. 'Do we still have them?'
'Yes, they're in the wardrobe in the spare bedroom, but nowadays you find it so much easier to put on a CD – and you don't have to keep getting up to turn them over. Most of them last over an hour. You can get your old vinyl out if you like, but we're not trying to revive your memories for the seventies, are we? For now, try the newer stuff and see if it awakens anything. You like that latest Nancy Wilson CD. Some of her stuff is quite soulful. You bought it cheap from the internet and you've been very pleased with it. I'll show you how to work the player.'
She demonstrated and he was impressed that he could use the remote control to operate the machine and the CD player displayed which track was playing. He squinted to read the card inside the case.
'When did I last have my eyes tested?' he asked.
'Only about two months ago,' she replied.
'Why am I struggling with some things, then?'
'You're wearing varifocals so that you see distances as well as being able to read close up. They just take a little getting used to. Just tip your head up when reading and use the bottom of the lenses.'
'So they're a bit like bi-focals, then?'
'Yeah, but without the harsh line.'

‘That explains why I was struggling when I came out of the hospital. I thought my injury was making me dizzy. My father used to have two pairs of glasses. He was always struggling to find one of his pairs. These are more convenient.’
’I like this one,’ Julie said, referring to the music that was playing.
Rob nodded in a non-committal way. ‘It’s a Bill Withers song. I prefer his version. I hope I’ve still got it.’
‘You know we went to see him back in the eighties,’ Julie said. ‘He appeared in Peterborough.’
‘Really? I’ve never seen anyone live.’ He had, of course seen several acts, but he wasn’t aware of the fact. ‘What was he like?’
‘He was brilliant, but the theatre was half-empty. It hadn’t been advertised very well, but it didn’t stop him giving a great show.’
‘I wish I could remember that,’ Rob said wistfully.
‘You will do one day,’ Julie said, returning to her work.

As they both sat down to a lunch of ham and cheese sandwiches, Julie asked ‘Has the music revived anything?’
‘No, I’m afraid not, but I did have an idea. We must have lots of photographs taken during our marriage. Perhaps I could scroll through some of them.’
‘That’s an excellent idea,’ she said. ‘The more recent ones, especially of the grandchildren, are on the computer. The older ones are in albums. I’ll dig some out before I get back to work. I need to work undisturbed this afternoon. I have to do the half-yearly appraisals. I hate that job.’
‘What are appraisals?’ he asked. He was getting rather fed up with having to keep asking questions but he

desperately wanted to come to terms with the twenty-first century.
'I sometimes wonder,' she replied. 'We have to review the progress of each of my staff. We have to set them objectives and discuss how well they are doing to achieve those objectives. Their progress will affect their pay increases at review time.'
'So, it's a bit like the school reports,' Rob said.
She laughed.' That's a very good analogy – must try harder! Anyway, as I said, I mustn't be disturbed – at least not until it's time for you to make a cup of tea. And you need to cook our meal this evening.'
'Me? Cook? I can't cook; unless you want cheese on toast!' His mother had always cooked for him and the only time his father had attempted to do so when was his mother had to go into hospital for a few days. It was a huge relief when she returned to resume her duties before she was really fit to do so.
'You can cook,' Julie said. 'You often rustle up something for us.' She sighed. 'When are you going to get back to normal? It'll have to be a jacket potato in the microwave.'

After lunch, Rob sat down with the photograph albums which Julie had chosen. There were three of them. One represented the best of their photographic efforts throughout the earlier years of their marriage and the other two were one for each of their children. She explained that the photos of the grandchildren were all digital and that they had stopped using old-fashioned albums well before then.
Before looking at the photographs, he selected another CD as background music. He picked up one by Bob James and Earl Klugh. He remembered a sixties record by Bob & Earl called *Harlem Shuffle*, which he liked.

Could this be the same pair? As the CD started playing, it was clear that it wasn't the same two people as this was jazz, but he found himself enjoying it, just as he had with most of Nancy Wilson's album which was a far cry from the material she recorded in the sixties.
He was keen to look at the photos of Sarah first of all. They were mostly in chronological sequence, starting with a tiny little thing with eyes almost closed, being held by a very proud father. He felt a lump in his throat to think that he and Julie had produced this little tiny bundle. There was a date hand-written beneath – April 7th 1990. That meant Sarah was now 29 years old.
As he perused the pages, further dates and captions had been added. There were several pages dated 1990, but gradually as Sarah had aged, the number of photos for each year decreased. There were a small number where Julie was holding Sarah. Rob thought his wife looked gorgeous. He could see a strong likeness to how Sarah looked at her current age. One showed Julie wearing a tight sweater. He couldn't take his eyes off it. Her breasts had probably been enlarged during her pregnancy.
Eventually, he forced himself to turn the page to find a photograph of his mother with a one year old Sarah perched on her lap. This was labelled 1991. His mother looked heavier and greyer than he remembered and he felt another lump in his throat. He had no memory of his mother during the last forty years and now she and his father had left this world. So many other relatives must have also joined her and Kate in whatever place dead people reside. He could feel a tear coming so he turned the page again.
Each person who appeared in the subsequent pages was slowly aging, including himself. The only person who seemed to improve with age was Sarah who gradually emerged through the various stages of

childhood to adolescence and the blossoming of her own beauty. That was where the album ended, presumably because these digital images that Julie had mentioned, had replaced them. He had noticed that pictures of Julie seldom appeared towards the end. Perhaps there would be more in the other two albums.
He reached for Ben's album. The first page said 'Born March 29th 1987.' So Ben was now thirty two years old. The quality of the first few photographs was not as high as those in Sarah's album. Rob guessed that they must have upgraded their camera at some point soon after Ben's birth because the quality did soon improve. As with Sarah's album, there were pictures of both Julie and Rob holding him and this time both of Rob's parents appeared. There were two other elderly people in the album so he assumed these were Julie's parents. There were also a few showing Ben tentatively clutching his baby sister, looking so pleased with himself. The pattern of people gradually appearing to age followed a similar one to Sarah's album.
By the time he had reached the last page, the music had long since finished. He hadn't noticed which at least, in his eyes, meant he hadn't found the jazz to be too intrusive.
He looked at his watch. It wasn't yet three o'clock. Julie had left him instructions to make a pot of tea some time between three and three thirty. Should he make it now? He didn't want her to snap at him again, but he had been wondering if he had turned into one of those hen-pecked husbands who couldn't stand up to their wives. If so, now was a good time to rectify the situation. He would play one more CD and finish looking at the photographs. He selected a CD by Grover Washington Jr. He had heard a little of his music because he knew he had recorded on the Motown label which leant a little credibility in Rob's eyes even though it was still jazz

albeit with a bit of a funky beat. In fact, Rob loved his version of Marvin Gaye's *Mercy, Mercy Me.*
The album he chose was called *Winelight* and on the cover was a picture of a glass of white wine positioned in front of a saxophone. He thought it was most effective, but even more effective was the music that emanated from the speakers. From the very first few beats, his feet were tapping and his head swaying to the rhythm even though this was a far cry from being dance music. Then the saxophone kicked in. Grover was caressing the melody in much the same way that a singer like Roberta Flack would phrase her lyrics. He wasn't blasting the notes out like so many other saxophone players. He was feeling each musical phrase as though serenading a young lady. Even as the tune reached a middle break, there was none of the usual weird jazz improvisations that occur in so many jazz records and when the main melody resumed, Rob felt a wave of pleasure that he'd never known from an instrumental before. When that first track was over, he wanted to play it again but another delightful tune began; perhaps not as good as *Winelight,* but still a cut above anything else he had heard that day. This continued throughout the whole album and he lost track of time, especially when Bill Withers started singing *Just the Two of Us* and yet there was still one more brilliant relaxing tune to finish up.
He realised that while this CD had been playing, he had been holding the photograph album but without even opening it. He looked at his watch. It was well after three thirty. He was in danger of being chastised for not making the tea, but he didn't care.
'I just wanted to finish that CD,' he said as he entered the adjoining room. 'I hope I haven't kept you waiting too long.'

'That's quite all right. I know that's one of your favourites,' she said. 'I like it as well. Any luck with memories?'
'No ... sorry.'

Chapter 11

Rob sat down with his cup of tea and the third photograph album. Another CD was playing in the background. This time, he had chosen the Philadelphia International mixture, feeling that he wanted to hear something more familiar, even though there were a few tracks he'd never heard before.

In this third photograph album, the photos seemed to be of a higher quality right from the very first picture, making him think that this was the point when they had upgraded their camera. There were no dates or captions and the subjects were varied. Some were of a garden, presumably their first together, including close up pictures of colourful flowers. There were also local scenes which he mostly recognised. One showed him wearing Polaroid clip-ons, sat on the harbour wall at Wells-Next-The-Sea and trying to look cool. Another one was of Julie from a different angle. None of these provoked memories and he desperately wished they did because they looked like happy times together.

As he waded through the album, he noticed that there were very few photographs of people and there were no signs of an actual holiday; probably just days out in various locations. There were some of stately homes that he did not recognise which was hardly surprising because he had never visited any before 1979. He had, however, been to Castle Acre Priory where he had once taken Kate for a delightful visit. He remembered how they had both commented on the sanctity and restfulness of the impressive ruins. The pictures of the priory brought back memories but not the ones Julie expected of him.

Towards the end of the album, there were some more seaside snaps. He guessed that these were taken in and around Cromer because he recognised the distinctive pier. One particularly artistic scene showed a figure gazing out to a dappled sky in the west, most probably taken at the end of the day as the shadows were lengthening. The figure was an overweight lady, he guessed in her forties. There was something familiar about her. Could this have been Julie's sister, perhaps? No, it was Julie. But surely she hadn't looked so heavy in any of the other photographs, not that there had been any of her in the last dozen or so pages. With no dates or captions, he had no sense of time for this picture. If, indeed, this was her, and it certainly looked like it, she had done well to lose the excess weight since then. He flicked through the last few pages hoping to see evidence of her weight loss, but there were no more people apart from a few distant strangers milling around a moated Elizabethan style building.

He wanted to know more about Julie's up and down figure, but how could he word it tactfully? She was still working so he had a little time to consider his approach. Meanwhile, he flipped through each of the albums again, hoping to see something that might trigger a memory, but to no avail.

He looked at his watch. It was after five o'clock. Julie was still working and the CD was still playing. It had started before four o'clock, so Julie had been right about some CDs lasting over an hour. With two tracks to go, this album would have lasted over seventy five minutes – and he never had to get up to turn it over.

He heard Julie close her laptop in the next room and let out a huge sigh. 'Thank God for that,' she said. 'That's over for another six months. I think it's time to make some tea, but I need to sit down and have a rest first.'

She joined him in the sitting room. 'I don't suppose we've roused any memories for you?'

He didn't mention the recollections of Kate. 'No, but I found it all interesting. Was that Cromer pier with that nice atmospheric skyline? It's a lovely picture.'
'Yes, I didn't want to include it in the album with me looking so huge, but you persuaded me that it was a lovely photo – despite my bulk! It was seeing that picture that made me do something about it.'
'What do you mean?' he asked.
'I've always had problems with my weight. Before we had the children, I was quite sporty,' she said. 'I played netball and hockey regularly and stayed around twelve stone. That may sound a lot, but I am tall and then there are these.' She cupped her impressive breasts and Rob stared at them, feeling that she had brought them to his attention so it was only polite to have a good look. She was wearing a checked blouse with breast pockets that seemed to be fighting to restrain her appendages. 'They must weigh a bit,' she added, 'and then there's my arse. That's worth a few kilos.'
Rob noticed that she was mixing metric and imperial weights. He didn't know how much a kilo was. It had taken him a few years to get used to decimalisation but in 1979, most people still used feet and inches and pounds and ounces.
Julie continued. 'Anyway, after each birth, I piled on the pounds and I was no longer doing any sport. You told me you didn't mind because it meant there was more of me to love, but I became quite miserable for a while, so I tried dieting. It worked well to start with, and I lost a few pounds, but then, after a few weeks, I started levelling out even though I was sticking to the diet. I knew that eating lettuce and crisp-bread for the rest of my life was not very healthy so the diet lapsed. Of course, now we know why the diet was no good, don't we?'
'Do we?' he asked.

'It's all to do with metabolics, isn't it?'
'Metal what?' he said on cue.
'This is the way you described it to me,' she said. 'When you take in less food, your metabolic rate slows down. It's like on *Star Trek* when they need to conserve energy. They lower the *life support systems*. That's what the body does if it's getting fewer nutrients. Lowering your metabolism means you're using less energy and therefore burning less fat, which is why you no longer lose weight. When you stopped playing football and started going to the gym, you borrowed a book from the library and learnt all about exercise and nutrition. You persuaded me to join a gym. At first, I was reluctant because I didn't want to build big muscles, but you pointed out that you don't build big muscles unless you really want to. So I was using the treadmills, the cycles and every machine in the gym until I worked out what was best for me. At first, it was hard work, but nowadays, I enjoy it.'
'That's why you've got such a great figure,' he said feeling his lust rising.
'Well, I don't know about that, but I don't look like a beached whale anymore.'
'Perhaps we should drive over to Cromer and take another photograph so we can have a "before and after" comparison,' Rob said.
'Perhaps we will some time,' she said. 'It might even revive some memories. I'd better get our meal on the go.'

The next morning, while they were eating breakfast, Julie said 'That's three nights in a row. I think that's more than we did when we first got married.'
Rob smiled. 'You have to remember that for me, I've never been married before so this is great – and we

don't have to worry about unwanted pregnancies. In a way, it must be better than the first few days of marriage.'

'Mmm ... I don't know about that. You managed three times on our wedding night. Anyway, I thought we'd go into town this morning. We need some groceries and you can see if Stamford looks at all familiar. If that doesn't work, this afternoon we'll have a little walk around the village. It will do you no harm to get a little exercise. You've been stuck indoors since Sunday.'

'There is one thing ...' he said. 'I'm not sure if it's relevant, but I had a funny dream last night. It's all a bit vague now, but I was in a big building, working, and I couldn't get out. I had these earphone things wrapped around my head. I needed the toilet, but there weren't any, so I did it under my desk and no one seemed to mind. Eventually, when it was dark, I went to get into my car, but I couldn't find it anywhere so I walked home. It was miles away and dark. My legs wouldn't move. The next thing I knew, I was on a bike ... still trying to get home. That's all I remember.'

'Well, you did work in a big building when you worked in the call centre and you probably wore headphones when answering the calls, so perhaps the memories are trying to come out even if it's only in your sleep. And you used to hate that drive home from Peterborough to Lynn; especially when you worked shifts and had to come home in the dark. I don't know about a bike, though. But it's a start, isn't it? Then there was that thing when you were reading *Ivor the Engine.* I wonder if we could find a hypnotist.'

The next morning, as they pulled into the supermarket car park, Julie said 'We need to remember what time we drove in. We've got just two hours to go around

town and get our shopping from the supermarket. They've got number plate recognition working here now. If we go over two hours we'll get a hefty fine. I think it's sixty pounds.'
'Sixty pounds?' he said incredulously. 'Who's recording the number plates?'
'There's a camera recording it as we drive in and out. They've got software to check it all.'
'How will they know it's our car?' he asked.
'Because they'll search the DVLA's database for our registration. The camera will read it again when we leave and I think that we can't return for at least another hour.'
'This is like *1984,*' he said. '*Big Brother* is watching you. Do they have *thought police* as well?'
'Not yet, but they will soon, I'm sure,' she said. 'There are cameras everywhere these days. It doesn't seem to stop the criminals, though. The police are too busy making sure you don't verbally offend anyone, but let's not go into all that. Just remember the time we drove in.'
Before setting off towards the shops, she went to the cash machine to fetch some cash. The evening before, she had patiently explained to Rob the use of debit and credit cards for paying for goods to avoid carrying large sums of money. He was amazed at the principal of contactless payments or using PIN numbers without needing to sign for anything. Naturally, he couldn't remember any of his numbers so Julie told him that if he needed to buy anything, she would do it for him. She handed him a ten pound note in case he wanted to buy something of small value. He felt like he was receiving some pocket money to buy sweets as his mother might have done all those years ago.
They were soon walking through Red Lion Square and on up High Street. A little way along, they were stopped

by a slim young lady wearing jeans with ragged knees. 'Rob! How are you? You're up and about, I see,' she said. 'Does that mean the fitness session for next week is back on?'
Of course Rob had no idea who she was, but it was easy to guess that she was one of his regular clients. 'Not yet, I fear,' he mumbled like a shy adolescent. 'I have to wait for the doctors to give me the go ahead.'
He wondered if Julie knew who the lady was, but if she did, she showed no signs of recognition and, for the moment, made no effort to join the conversation.
'What is the problem?' the young lady said '... if it's not too personal, that is?'
Rob wasn't sure how he should respond. After all, this was his livelihood and he didn't want her to think that he could no longer fulfil his role. 'Just a little injury,' he replied, hoping his vagueness might persuade her that it was a little personal.
'Do you know how long it will be?' she asked.
'Let's see what the doctor says,' said Julie in an impatient tone. 'Are you one of the ladies I called on Monday?'
'Yes, I'm Becky.'
'Well, we'll be in touch when we know more. We have to get along before we get a parking fine.' and she hurried Rob along the road.
It was silly, she knew, but she felt a twinge of jealousy. She was sure that the sixty year old Rob would never stray with another woman, but this Rob, with the mind of a twenty year old, might consider Becky more appealing than a woman in her late fifties despite their recent satisfying night-time activities.
Rob was more concerned about losing his clients since that was his means of earning a living. He felt that Julie had talked down to the young lady like an aged school

teacher and he didn't feel that had been necessary, if not actually injurious to his profession.
Julie headed for the M&S store at the far end of High Street and went into the ladies' clothing section. 'I want to see if I can find a new top,' she said.
'I'll have a wander around the men's section,' Rob responded, looking around.
'There isn't a men's section here,' she said. 'It's only a small store. Just wait outside if you don't want to hang around with me in here.' Like most men, Rob felt uncomfortable standing around in a woman's clothing department.
He did as his wife suggested and had a look down the street. He hadn't spent any of his "pocket money" and was tempted to go and buy some sweets just to make a point, but he wasn't sure where. He hadn't seen any sweet shops and, surprisingly, no tobacconists, but there seemed to be a plethora of charity shops. He liked the architecture of the varied buildings above the shop fronts. The stonework was like nothing he had ever seen in Norfolk, but it did resemble some of the houses in his new village.
A few minutes later, Julie reappeared. 'Nothing in my size that I like,' she said.
'I like this stonework in a lot of the buildings,' he said.' Is that a local stone?'
'I would think so,' she said. 'There's a thing called Barnack Stone and another called Ketton Stone. They're both local villages – and then there is Collyweston Slate on some of the roofs. There are a lot of cottages in our village built like that. This afternoon, we will have a wander around our village. It might stir some memories. Does Stamford look at all familiar?'
'No, I'm sure I would have remembered this. It's very nice, but I can't say the shops inspire me. I haven't seen a record shop.'

‘I’m not sure there’s ever been a record shop – at least, not while we’ve lived here. Even Peterborough has now only got one store that I know of, but the charity shops often have some records and CDs ... but you’ve got enough. We’re running out of storage space for any more.’
‘There are certainly plenty of charity shops to explore,’ he said. ‘And what’s with all these coffee shops? Is that what people are holding in their hands as they walk down the street?’
‘Yes, it seems to be what people do these days. You and I like to sit down and enjoy our coffee and in my mind, it never tastes so nice out of these plastic mugs they use, but that’s just my opinion.’
Rob remembered a coffee bar in King’s Lynn where young people would regularly meet up. ‘Do people meet up in these coffee shops?’ he asked.
‘You and I never use the ones in Stamford,’ Julie replied. ‘If we want a coffee, we just go home and make one and save our money. I never understand what’s so special about these places, myself. We’ve had a coffee in other towns and I never noticed people meeting up, but I suppose some might.’
They didn’t linger too long in town. Julie was well organised with her supermarket shopping and they were soon home in time for a coffee before lunch – in a china mug!

Rob had never eaten quiche before. It still amazed him that, using the microwave oven, a portion could be heated up from chilled in just forty five seconds. The quiche reminded him a little of the egg and bacon pie he used to enjoy as school dinner at the King’s Lynn Grammar School. It had been his favourite meal there.

'You managed that walk around town all right, didn't you?' his wife said. 'You were on your feet for almost two hours. That's a good sign that you're on the mend. I'm sure you can manage another little walk this afternoon.'

'Yes, I feel fine, thank you. I'd like to see the village. What I've seen so far looks very nice.'

Chapter 12

'You'll need your walking shoes,' Julie said. 'At one point, the footpath goes across a field. It's probably going to be dry, but you don't want to mess up your boat shoes.'
So far, Rob had been wearing the same shoes he had worn to leave the hospital, which had seemed surprisingly comfortable and nothing like what he would have worn in 1979. He'd never heard of boat shoes. He was still relying on Julie to tell him what to wear each day until he became more familiar with his wardrobe and the location of his various items of clothing.
At first, they set out along the road they had previously travelled a few times in the car but now Rob was able to leisurely look around at his surroundings more closely. 'What are all those things on the roofs?' he asked.
'They're solar panels,' Julie replied. 'They generate electricity and supposedly save the owners lots of money in electricity costs.'
'They're ugly,' he said. 'Do they work?'
'Yes, but it depends on the weather – and it costs a lot of money to install, so it takes many years to recoup the costs.'
They carried on and came to a bridge over an attractive stream and they lingered to enjoy it for a while. The stream seemed to cut the village in two because it now seemed as though they were back in the countryside. They progressed to the southern section of the village and turned left, past a pub that offered food and drink, towards the church and an attractive little square where a red telephone box was now occupied by a defibrillator.
'What's that?' he asked.
'It's a defibrillator,' she said.

'Like the things they have in hospitals?' he asked.
'Yes. Most places now have one somewhere. It's a good use of the old telephone box, don't you think?'
'But what if someone wants to make a telephone call?'
'Everyone has a mobile these days,' she said, '... well, not everyone, but these boxes were just getting vandalised so BT decommissioned nearly all of them. I've seen some villages use them for miniature libraries. People leave books that they've finished reading for others to borrow.'
Almost opposite the church was a farm with chickens and guinea fowl roaming around and a large pig snuffling by the fence. It seemed strange to see a farm in the midst of the habitations, but with the stream bisecting the village, it almost made sense. The land either side of the stream looked unsuitable for housing.
Church Lane turned into The Street, which he thought was an unimaginative name for a road. When they turned the corner into Pinfold Lane, they saw a building called *The Farm* which made them both laugh. It would have been even more amusing had *The Farm* been on *The Street*, but it wasn't.
'How are you feeling?' Julie asked as they moved down the lane.
'I'm fine, thank you. I'm enjoying seeing the village.'
'Yes, we're lucky to live around here.' He sensed she wanted to broach a delicate matter. 'So you won't mind if I leave you on your own on Monday. I've got to go into work for a meeting. I could take you with me and leave you in reception, but that wouldn't be a lot of fun for you, would it?'
'No, I'll be all right,' he said. At last he could be trusted with his own company. He could amuse himself with the television and some more CDs. 'But what about getting my bandage changed?'

‘We’ll have time for that,’ she replied. ‘My meeting is at ten o’clock. I won’t be back for lunch so you can make yourself a sandwich. There’s a fresh loaf in the freezer.’
‘Can you buy frozen bread now?’ he asked with surprise.
‘Of course not,’ she replied trying not to laugh. ’You put it in the freezer when it’s still fresh and defrost it when you need it. It will stay fresh in the freezer for ages. Are you happy to be on your own for a few hours?’
‘Yeah, I’ll be all right,’ he repeated as they turned up a footpath alongside a pond. It was a pleasant enough pond with benches and walkways but not as nice as the pond at South Wootton where he and Kate would often feed the ducks. A lone mallard swimming away from them didn’t do much to alter his opinion and the old feelings of grief returned for a while.
They soon emerged back onto The Street where they had been minutes before.
‘We’re back here,’ he said waking from his self-pity. ‘That was a short walk.’
‘We’re going to turn off again.’ She said. ‘We’ve done this walk dozens of times. We zigzag through the village to cover all the little footpaths and still see all the nice old cottages.’ At the pleasant square near the church, she led them down another footpath and they were soon crossing a footbridge over the same stream they had passed earlier.
‘This is a lovely stream,’ he said. ‘Does it have a name?’
‘Not that I know of,’ she replied, ‘but it does flow into The Chater a little further down.’
‘I’ve never heard of The Chater,’ he said. He always thought he was good at geography, but then he’d never studied Rutland at school.

'It's a nice little river ... mostly a stream really. It goes on through Ketton and, just beyond, it joins the Welland.'
'I've heard of The Welland,' he said, feeling pleased with himself. 'It's one of the rivers that drain into The Wash. There's the Welland, The Nene and The Great Ouse. We learnt all about it at the Grammar School.'
'Yeah, you were always good at Geography, especially when we play *Trivial Pursuit* with the family.'
'What ...?'
'It's a board game,' she said anticipating the question.
'I can't wait to play it,' he said. 'Although there seem to be so many ways of entertaining yourself these days ... all those television channels; music on miniature discs, cameras in phones. What else have I yet to discover?'
They took another diversion. This time along a path which led onto a pasture that sloped down to the little stream they had already crossed twice. Rob noticed the horses in the far corner and wondered if he and his wife were safe, but the footpath was well trodden and he assumed the owner of the horses would not have let them roam free if they were dangerous. He found himself caring for Julie's safety and he wondered how fast she could run if it became necessary.
'We've walked across this field dozens of time,' she said sensing his slight hesitation. 'I don't suppose you remember the time we were chased by the cows in the next field, do you?'
'Cows?' he said. 'They're usually harmless. Are you sure they weren't bullocks?'
'No, they were cows,' she said. 'They had some calves with them. Some idiot was exercising his dog in the same field. Cows don't like dogs, especially when they have young. The dog was running around loose and although the owner tried to call him back, the dog was having too much fun to take any notice and when the

cows started getting fidgety, the dog probably thought they were having a game, but they started stampeding. We only just got out of the field in time. At least, we were all right. The dog owner ran to the gate at the far end. We assumed he made it. We ran to the one at this end. All those hours on the treadmill paid off that day. I don't think I would have made it if I had still been obese. Do you remember it at all?'

'No, it sounds very scary,' he said. 'Cows are big beasts. They are usually peaceful but I'm sure they could do some damage.'

'I think they would have got you first as you kept hanging back to protect me like a big hero, but most of the cows chased the other man and his dog. I like to think he learned a lesson about dogs and cattle. It certainly scared us. None of this has struck a chord with you, then?'

'I'm afraid not,' he said. 'Is that the field you're talking about?' He was pointing to a field the other side of the road they had just reached.

'Yes, but we haven't really got time to go along that one today. I have to get our tea ready before we go babysitting. We need to head along this road back towards our house. Sarah and Neville are going to see *Twelfth Night* at Tolethorpe and they want to go early to have a picnic with some friends.'

As they neared their home, Rob asked 'What made us choose this house?'

'It was what we could afford at the time – and what was available. Don't you like it?'

'Yes, of course,' he said. After all, it was wonderful compared to his parent's old house in Norfolk with its inadequate coal fire, draughty doors and windows and lack of parking space, but he had liked the look of the old stone cottages in South Luffenham.

‘At the time,’ she added, ‘you were still working in the call centre and it had been a struggle financially. In fact, we’ve nearly always struggled, but we’re all right now – as long as you can get back to work soon. I earn good money and I should get a good pension when I retire at 67.’
’67?’ he exclaimed. ‘Why can’t you retire at 60?’
‘Because they’ve changed the retirement age for men and women,’ she said. ‘Some people can still retire at 66. It depends when you were born, but for me and you, it’s 67. The country could no longer afford the old retirement ages. People are living so much longer these days.’
Rob let out a sigh. ‘I thought that scientists claimed that in the future, we would have more leisure time and could enjoy retiring earlier, not later.’

Before venturing out for their babysitting duties, Julie still had enough time to cook a delicious meal for them both. That morning, she had bought some good quality turkey mince and, following a recipe from one of her cookery books, had produced some meatballs flavoured with garlic and spices. It was served on a bed of pasta, garnished with a tomato based sauce.
Rob complimented her on her work, telling her it was the best meal he could remember eating, which didn’t necessarily mean a great deal since his memory didn’t cover the last forty years.
‘The recipe was for four people,’ she said, ‘so there are still enough left over for another meal. Do you have any suggestions how I might serve them?’
‘How about in a French Maid’s outfit,’ he said.
She didn’t laugh but was pleased that his sense of humour had returned.

'Nanny! Nanny!' cried both the children as Rob and Julie entered Sarah's house in Ketton.
'Hello, my darlings. What have you all been up to?' Julie asked.
Belinda was first and delivered a lengthy tirade about all the things she had been doing that afternoon, most of which revolved around Elsa, the character from *Frozen.*
'What about you, Barney?' Rob asked after a few minutes, feeling that both he and Barney hadn't yet managed to get a word in.
'Well ...' he started, but Belinda was off again giving Barney little chance to say anything.
Just then, Neville appeared carrying a large hamper.
'Do you need a hand? Rob asked, feeling that he needed a rest from hearing about Elsa.
'No worries,' Neville replied, struggling out of the door towards their car. Rob had never heard the expression before. Why would there be any worries?
Sarah appeared carrying a canvas bag with more goodies for their picnic. 'Belinda's had her bath so she's ready to go to bed at six thirty. Barney had a bath last night and he goes to bed at seven. There are some bottles of Aspells in the fridge if you want a drink.'
'What's Aspells?' Rob asked.
'It's our favourite cider,' Julie replied.
'I don't drink cider,' Rob said. 'Do you have any beer?'
'Yes, there are some beers,' Sarah said. 'I thought you liked Aspells?'
'He does,' said Julie. 'He just doesn't know he does. We'll be fine. You get off and enjoy yourselves.'

'We will,' said Sarah. 'We're meeting Sandy there. They live in Belmesthorpe, so they're coming from the other direction.'
'Just time for a quick story, then,' said Julie to the two children.
'I want to watch *Paw Patrol*,' said Barney.
'Yeah, *Paw Patrol*,' echoed Belinda.
'That's on YouTube,' said Sarah. 'You know how to find that on the television, don't you?'
'Yes, I'm sure we can manage that. We have YouTube on our set,' Julie said.
As usual, Rob had no idea what they were talking about, but he was busy admiring his beautiful clever daughter and was still bothered by his thoughts about her.
'Have you got something to wear if it turns a bit chilly later?' Julie asked her daughter 'When we went, it turned very cold after the interval and we had to huddle together to keep warm.'
'Yes, I've put a jumper in my bag,' Sarah replied. 'We'd better get going,' and she gave each of her children a big hug and told them to be good.
'Did we go to see a Shakespeare play?' Rob asked after Sarah had left. He had never appreciated the nation's acclaimed playwright and couldn't imagine attending a play voluntarily.
'No, we went to see them perform *Dad's Army*. It was mostly the same script as the TV series, but it was well produced and we enjoyed it – except when it started raining heavily. We were all right because we were under cover but the actors are in the open and they were soaked, but they carried on. We couldn't hear what they were saying because of the noise of the rain, but we already knew the script anyway so it didn't matter. Each year, I think they perform two

Shakespeare plays and one other. They're doing *Blythe Spirit* this year.'
'Nanny, are we going to watch *Paw Patrol*?' Belinda asked impatiently.
'Yes, my darling – if I can remember how to find it. Grandad usually manages but he can't remember at the moment.' Julie didn't bother to ask for Rob's help as she knew the outcome.
She fiddled with the remote control for several minutes and was starting to get exasperated.
'Can't you just key in a channel number?' Rob suggested, trying to be of use.
'No, it's not on a channel number,' she replied sharply. 'It's ... oh, I don't know what it is. Ah, what's this?'
'*Paw Patrol*!' shouted Barney. 'That's it, Nanny.'
They all sat down together; Belinda on her Nanny's lap and Barney on the floor right in front of the set.
Rob was not impressed. He felt the programme was too American for his liking, but then he remembered how he used to enjoy *The Flintstones* and *Yogi Bear.*
The children wanted to watch a second episode but Julie insisted that it was time for Belinda to go to bed and turned off the television. 'I'll read you a story in your bedroom,' she said. 'Meanwhile, Grandad can read *Ivor the Engine* to Barney.'
'I don't want *Ivor the Engine,*' said Barney.
'But it might make Grandad better,' she said. 'You remember that he had a nasty bang on the head? He's been a bit poorly ever since. Reading *Ivor* helps him.'
'Can't you give him Calpol?' Barney said. 'That's what mum gives me when I'm poorly.'
'I don't think Calpol works on Grandads. You want him to get better, don't you?'
'I s'pose so,' he said and fetched the book from his little chest of books. He then plonked himself on Rob's lap as Julie took Belinda up to bed.

As Rob started reading, he noticed that the light in that position was not good for reading and he remembered Neville suggesting he should turn on the lamp. What was the command he issued? 'Alexis, would you turn on the light.'
Nothing happened. He repeated the command. Barney helped him out. 'You need to say *Alexa,* Grandad' he said.
'Alexa, turn on the light.'
'Okay,' came the reply from the hidden device, but it was the main light that lit up not the standard lamp behind them and this caused less than helpful shadows on the book.
He tried again. 'Alexa, turn on the lamp behind us.'
'I'm sorry, I don't understand that command,' she said.
'Alexa, turn on the silly lamp.'
'I'm sorry, I don't understand that command,' she repeated.
'Alex, please turn on the lamp.'
'Okay.' This time, it worked. She obviously didn't like bad tempered commands and good manners always help.
He read the story much as he done two days earlier, but this time nothing seemed to stir in his memory despite the circumstances being almost identical.
'Why are you using that funny voice?' Barney asked as he done before.
'I told you. It's because it's set in Wales and Welsh people talk with an accent.'
Barney laughed and that gave Rob a warm feeling.
After a second reading, Julie reappeared. 'She seems to have settled. How are you two men getting on? Has *Ivor* had any effect?'
'Not this time,' replied Rob. 'I think I may have been trying too hard to remember things. I'm not sure it works that way.'

‘That’s a shame,’ she said. ‘I think a trip over to King’s Lynn would be a good idea, but maybe we should wait until you’ve seen the doctor again. Now is this little boy just about ready for bed?
‘I want another story,’ Barney responded.
‘Well, why don’t we take one upstairs and I’ll read it to you up there?’
‘Oh, all right. Can you do funny voices like Grandad?’
‘I’ll try.’

Chapter 13

Julie was up early the next morning. She said she wanted to get to the gym before everyone else starting hogging the machines. As she departed, Rob was still feeling a little disappointed that she had declined his sexual advances the night before. She had told him that she was feeling too tired for all that. What was the point of being married, he thought, if you couldn't have sex whenever you wanted? Julie had correctly pointed out to him that he had done very well since leaving hospital, but he shouldn't overdo it. Nevertheless, he still found that sleeping next to a woman was too much like all his dreams had come true and in the seventies, every opportunity had been precious.

So with Julie out of the house, he occupied his morning by watching old recorded episodes of quiz programmes on the television. He considered that the questions might help him learn a few things about his new world. He started with *The Chase* which intrigued him and annoyed him in roughly equal measures. Many of the questions were outside his dated sphere of knowledge and, indeed, interest, but those relating to history and geography were mostly better for him. Some of the competitors seemed ill equipped to appear on a quiz show and he wondered why they would chose to embarrass themselves in that way, but receiving a thousand pounds for each correct answer must have been enticing.

Some of them couldn't even speak properly, ending each sentence in a questioning tone like an Australian. 'So, I work in Haitch Har?' one said. Rob remembered Julie's disparaging comments about her own HR colleagues and it was clear to him that you didn't need to speak properly to work in *Haitch Har.*

'What do you do in your spare time?' the host asked.

'So, myself and my partner like going on holiday?'
'You don't start a sentence with *myself.*' Rob said out loud. 'And how is going on holiday something you do in your spare time?' He also disapproved of the constant need to open a sentence with the word "so."
Some of the contestants managed to omit verbs and pronouns in their answers.
'Big fan of Rugby,' one answered. 'Like going to gigs.'
Rob's English teacher, Mr Gregory, from the Grammar School in King's Lynn, would have been appalled.
The host was also guilty of bad grammar. 'If you *was* to win some money today ...' he asked.
'WERE!' Rob shouted at the screen. 'If you WERE to win some money ...'
Nevertheless, he enjoyed the show and thought Bradley Walsh was quite witty, although Rob was sure that Hughie Green would never have tried to belittle the contestants the way the Chaser did.
Having won three thousand pounds, the first contestant could have won even more, but, for some inexplicable reason, decided to gamble it all by answering some further questions for the same amount. Why didn't he just take the money and leave? Three thousand pounds was a lot of money. By the end of the show, no one had won any money.
Rob then watched an episode of *Pointless.* In this show, the contestants were playing for much less money, but if they failed, they could come back for another show. If they won, they might still leave the show empty handed and were not allowed to return. That didn't seem fair to him. Failure was being rewarded, but at least the contenders were not belittled by the quizmasters – indeed, quite the opposite as Alexander Armstrong seemed genuinely upset when each pair of contestants was asked to leave, even though that was what the show was all about.

Just as the programme ended, Julie re-appeared, looking enticing in her leggings. She sat beside him and asked what he had been watching. She then told him that he usually rooted for the Chaser and he wasn't surprised at that statement.
'What exercises do you do in the gym?' he asked as he turned off the set.
She told him about the various cardio- and resistance exercises, all of which meant little to him, so she demonstrated her favourite which involved her thighs and buttocks, and needless to say, he soon had an erection.
'Not now,' she said as his hands started to wander, but he was persistent. Twenty minutes later, she gathered up her clothes and told him to make coffee while she had a shower.

During the rest of that Sunday, Julie dealt with three incoming telephone calls, all for Rob. One was on their landline, the other two on his mobile which he still felt uncomfortable about answering. He still hadn't got into the habit of carrying it around with him. Two of the calls were from clients of his wanting to know if he would be back at work that week, which she duly dismissed firmly but politely with a promise to call when things changed.
The third call was from Rob's friend Jed, inviting him to go canoeing on Rutland Water. As Jed wasn't one of Rob's clients, she felt comfortable about telling him the full truth of Rob's injury. Jed offered to call round during the week to see if he might jog Rob's memory. Julie said that would be kind of him, but no date was agreed.
'That was your friend Jed,' she said to Rob when she had finished the call. 'He wanted to know if you wanted to go canoeing this week. I told him not this week while you still had your dressing on the wound. You don't

want to get that wet. He might call round one day. I don't suppose Jed's name means anything to you, does it?'
He shook his head. 'Canoeing?' he said. 'Do sixty year olds go canoeing? I'm not a very good swimmer, you know.'
He tried to imagine his father taking up such a pursuit. In 1979, his father would have only been in his mid-forties. He just about managed to ride his bike and Rob couldn't imagine him squeezing into a canoe.
'Where do we do this canoeing? On the Welland, I suppose.' He didn't think that there were any other local rivers big enough.
'No, you go to Rutland Water.'
'What's that?'
'It's a big reservoir. It's only just down the road. I'll take you there some time.'
'Who is this Jed?' Rob asked.
'You knew him from the Call Centre and you both got on really well. He lives in Empingham and introduced you to some of the local places of interest – mostly pubs, of course. He likes a drink or two. Empingham is handy for Rutland Water. You two are like Morecambe and Wise when you get together. Actually, now that I think about it, perhaps you should get together. As you're on your own tomorrow morning, why don't I ask him if he'd like to call round and catch up with each other?'
Rob hesitated. Just because a sixty year old version of himself gets on with this chap, doesn't mean that in his present state of mind, he would, but if it helped him restore even part of his memory, it would be worthwhile, so he agreed and Julie rang him back. It was soon agreed with Jed. If the weather was fine, they would sit in the back garden and look over the paddock,

but Jed was under orders not to take him anywhere else ... like the pub, or Rutland Water.

The nurse thought his wound was healing nicely and considered not replacing the dressing to let the air get to his wound, but Julie pointed out that the wound might weep a little onto the pillow and make a mess so he returned home with a new but smaller dressing, meaning he still couldn't wash his hair properly. It was now feeling itchy and looked dank and messy.
He had been impressed by the technology at the surgery where his name had been flashed up on a TV screen telling him to go to Room 21. This was nothing like the old doctors' waiting room in King's Lynn, but he assumed King's Lynn was now suitably updated as well.

It had been agreed that Jed would arrive between ten and eleven o'clock. At just before ten thirty, the door bell rang. Rob had been reading the newspaper and had not been expecting the chimes to actually be in the same room as him. This was the first time that anyone had called at their house since his release from hospital. His parents had never possessed a door bell and he had been expecting a knock on the door not a musical chime just a few feet from his ear.
He opened the front door and was surprised by the appearance of his friend. Jed was barely five foot six inches tall, but squat and with a bullet shaped head that was close-shaven and tanned. This was a man who epitomised a healthy outdoor lifestyle. His appearance reminded Rob of someone, but he couldn't quite say

whom. The white tee shirt and sharply creased trousers added to the feeling of déjà vu.
'Hello Sunbeam,' Jed said, beaming like a cat from deepest Cheshire.
'You must be Jed,' Rob said.
'No, I'm the bloody Queen of Sheba. Of course I'm Jed. What the Hell have you been doing to yourself, you silly old sod. Are you going to invite me in or are we going stand on your doorstep all day?'
'Sorry. Yes, come in. I'm afraid I don't remember you at all – this bang on the head, you know.' He pointed to his head. 'But, maybe if we sit and talk for a while, something will come back to me.'
'Perhaps you need another bang on the head,' Jed said.
'I think that's just an old myth,' Rob said not realising that Jed was being flippant. 'It might do more harm than good one of the doctors said. Come out into the garden. Do you want a cup of coffee ... or tea, perhaps?'
'Tea?' Jed exclaimed. 'When have you ever known me to drink tea?'
'Er ... well, I've never know you to have anything, because I don't remember meeting you before. How do you have your coffee?'
'This really is like meeting a stranger,' Jed said. 'Black ... and none of your weedy decaff stuff, mind.' Jed didn't go into the garden. He remained standing in the kitchen as Rob made their drinks and continued talking.
'So, are you getting any treatment for this loss of memory?'
'Not at the moment. I've got an appointment at the hospital on Friday. I think they feel it will get better by itself – if not, they'll have to find some kind of specialist; though in what, I don't know. Julie thinks I need a

hypnotist or something, but where do you find them? In the Yellow Pages? Do they still have Yellow Pages?'
'Yeah, but it's all on-line, now,' Jed replied. 'This can't be a lot of fun for your lovely wife?'
'No, of course not,' Rob said. 'When I came round on Wednesday, I didn't know her. I thought it was still 1979.'
'1979 ... that's what, forty years? How can just forget forty years?'
'I know. Every now and then, I think something rings a bell, but it doesn't amount to anything. Speaking of which ... your surname's not Perry, is it?'
'Perry? Of course not! It's Wade. What made you think it was Perry?'
Rob smiled. 'It's just that you reminded me a little of my old Sports Master at school – just in looks and build. You see, I can remember everything prior to 1979 as clear as a bell.' He handed Jed's mug to him and added 'Let's go and sit outside, shall we?'
As they sat down at the patio table, Rob asked 'So we met at this call centre. Did we work closely together?'
'No, I was your manager. I employed you and taught you all about Customer Service. You were one of my best workers. Even though you had all that travelling, you were always the most reliable person in the team, and apart from one occasion when the A47 was closed due to an accident, you were always first to arrive in the morning. Mind you, you were always first out of the door as well. I don't blame you for that, with that long journey home. I was sorry to see you leave, but it all worked out for the best.'
'Do you still work there?' Rob asked.
'No, I took early retirement ... two years ago. I receive an army pension, so when the Government changed the retirement age, I decided I wasn't going to hang on

until I'm sixty seven. I want to enjoy my last years – and I do.'
'How long were you in the army?' Rob asked.
'Twenty five years. Twenty five glorious years.'
'Did you see any action?' Rob asked.
'The Falklands in 1982 ... a bloody affair. I lost a few friends in that.' He went quiet and, although Rob wanted to know more about the conflict, he decided to hold back. 'Then we were posted to Northern Ireland for a tour. That wasn't the sort of service that I signed up for. You expect that there was a chance of being sent off to a war, but that was not a very nice sort of war – if there is such a thing.'
Rob had forgotten about *The Troubles* and asked a very stupid question. 'Are we still fighting over there?'
'No, Rob. It's all changed now.' Jed's mood had altered completely. 'We had what is called *The Peace Agreement* which meant all those bastards that killed our soldiers and innocent people, are free ... and some of them managed to sit on the new devolved government. Just to add salt to the wounds, some of our brave soldiers are being charged with trumped up accusations of ... I don't want to talk about it, if you don't mind. Let's change the subject, shall we?'
'Of course; it's just that I think I need to know what's been happening in the last forty years. You probably think that I'm a complete ignoramus.'
'No, Rob. No one would ever call you that. I can't begin to understand what you're going through. This must be a completely different world to 1979.'
Rob nodded. 'You don't know the half of it. At times, it feels like an episode of *Star Trek.* It wouldn't surprise me to find we've got aliens living next door. What was it like at the call centre?'
'Pretty boring most of the time, if I'm honest. I always wanted to be a doctor, but I never had the patients.'

Rob was a little slow to react to his joke, but then started laughing. 'That reminds me of a chap I used to work with in Lynn,' he said. 'He told me he used to be an archaeologist but his career was in ruins.'
'Oh, great one, Rob,' Jed said with a grin. 'This is just like the old times – us telling each other jokes. I'm sure I've told you my doctor joke before, but if you don't remember it, I could recite my whole repertoire all over again and it would be like you hearing them for the first time.'
'Here's one,' said Rob. 'A ventriloquist was performing his act on stage. He said to his dummy "*Have you got a joke for me today, Archie?*" Archie, the dummy, replied "*There was this Irishman ...*"
'Just then, an Irishman in the audience stood up and said *"Hey ... Oi'm Irish and ..."*
Jed stopped him. 'I'm sorry, Rob. You're not allowed to tell jokes like that anymore. It's called racial stereotyping and it causes offence.'
'But I'm sure it was Frank Carson who told the joke in the first place – and he's as Irish as you can get, isn't he?'
'Yeah, it's probably not people like Frank that protest,' said Jed. 'It's all the liberal minded lefties who think they need to stand up for his interests. I agree with some of their principles, but everything's changed in the last few years – some things for the better; others completely over the top. And whatever you do, don't mention the 'N' word.'
Rob looked puzzled. 'The 'N' word? I don't know what that is. I know the 'F' word and the 'C' word.'
'Oh, they're all right now,' Jed said. 'You'll often hear them on the telly – should be after nine o'clock, of course. It's usually some talentless comedian who thinks if they add those words to what they're saying, it makes them sound funny and "down with the kids" but,

of course, they're really just trying to get some cheap laughs because they can't tell proper jokes. Frank Carson never resorted to swear words, but then, he told proper jokes. A lot of so called comedians just stand on stage and tell stories that enable them to put across their own political agenda.'

'So what's the 'N' word?' Rob asked.

'Let's just say, don't do *Eenie, Meenie, Miney, Mo,*' Jed replied.

'Oh, I see,' said Rob, remembering the same advice from Julie.

'Of course, if you're actually black,' said Jed, 'you can use the word. See what I mean? The world's gone mad.'

There was a lull in the conversation. Under normal circumstances, this would not have bothered either party. They would have sat together and just enjoyed the view over the paddock which at that moment didn't even have a horse to occupy their reverie, but now, they were like two complete strangers. Jed tried to think of something that might help jog Rob's memory. Rob tried to think of something that might involve their mutual interests, which as far as he knew was either canoeing or their old jobs at the Call Centre. He knew nothing about canoeing, so eventually, he asked 'What exactly did I do at the Call centre?'

'You answered calls,' Jed said flippantly, then added 'It was an insurance company and you dealt specifically with calls about home and contents insurance, mostly discussing queries about claims. It sounds a little boring, but each call was different. Sometimes, you might feel someone was making a fraudulent claim in which case, you would pass it on to a specialist who would investigate further. Does any of that ring a bell?'

'No,' he said shaking his head.

'Do you remember Big Brenda?' Jed said with a grin.

Rob shook his head but grinned as well as he expected a funny story and said 'How big was Big Brenda?'
'Not that big, but above average – and very tall. I don't suppose you remember Nice Eric, either?'
'No, why was he called Nice Eric?'
'Well, he wasn't exceptionally nice, but there was another chap called Eric as well ... and he wasn't very nice. He could be quite obnoxious at times. One day, you were talking about Eric and someone asked "Which Eric?" and you replied the nice one; so his name stuck.
'Anyway, Nice Eric was always quite quiet; a happily married man who kept himself to himself, but for some reason, Big Brenda was telling someone that she used to be a gymnast and could still put her legs behind her neck. What a thought, that was! Eric didn't believe her and told her to prove it. She said she wasn't going to do it in the office, especially as she wasn't dressed for the manoeuvre. Eric persisted and to save her any further hassle from Eric, you said you had seen her do it, so he had to believe it. I don't think you had seen her, but you just wanted to assure him that she wasn't lying and that was it at that time.
'But Eric went away and thought about it and a few days later, tried again to persuade her to demonstrate her flexibility, which I must admit, I'd have liked to have seen for myself. To cut a long story short, over the next few weeks, he became a real nuisance and she called him a pervert and threatened to report him to HR. This shook him up and he realised that perhaps it did sound a bit pervy, but instead of just forgetting about it, he sent her an e-mail apologising. She replied saying that she accepted his apology, but still considered him to be a pervert and didn't want anything to do with him. This bothered him even more and over the next few weeks, he sent her more e-mails trying to convince her that he wasn't what she said, but it only made matters worse.

You know the old expression – when in a hole, stop digging. Well, Eric took his digging too far and she complained about him to me and to HR. He was given a warning. He left a few months later. He said it wasn't connected but I think it had some bearing on his leaving – and we never did see Big Brenda with her legs around her neck; unless you can tell me different!'

Rob smiled. He thought it was a great story, but wished that he could remember the events for himself.

'What time are you expecting Jules back?' Jed asked.

Rob was taken aback by Jed's nickname for his wife. Then he remembered seeing 'Jools' come up on his phone when he was in the hospital. 'She didn't say,' he replied. 'She told me to make myself a sandwich for lunch, so I'm not expecting her before then.'

'We could nip down to the pub,' Jed said, 'but I was made to promise not to. I wouldn't want to get on the wrong side of your wife.' He was joking, but Rob took him at his word.

'Does she come across as that intimidating?' he asked.

'No, no ... I was just joking. She's a lovely lady – and you're a very lucky chap. I know she is anxious to look out for you in your current situation.'

'You don't think I'm hen-pecked, do you?'

'You? Hen-pecked? I wouldn't have thought so. You really aren't yourself at the moment, are you? Otherwise you wouldn't ask such a stupid question.'

Rob sighed. 'It may seem a stupid question to you, but I seem to be a different person to what I was in 1979 ... and I'm still getting to know my wife. It's all very strange.'

Jed nodded. 'I'm sure it will all sort itself out. The doctors can do wonderful things these days. If I can't take you down the pub today, I'd better get off and sort my own lunch out. I don't know how much good I've been, but if you like, I'll come around again in a few days. Give my love to Julie.'

Rob thanked him and showed him out. He had been tempted to ask Jed if he would like to join him in a sandwich, but he still didn't feel like this was his house to make free with his wife's bread and cheese.

Chapter 14

'What are you planning to do with yourself today?' Julie asked over breakfast the next day.
He sighed. 'Much the same as usual ... as I'm not allowed to drive or go out on my own.'
'Well, I think you could go out for a walk around the village. I'm sure you can remember the little walk we did last week. It will only take about half an hour, but at least you can get out and get some fresh air and exercise. As you managed all right on your own yesterday, I think I'll pop into work for a few hours. I'll come back in time for lunch. What do you think?'
'Yes, all right,' he said. Was he supposed to thank her? As a twenty year old, he could always become easily bored, but as a sixty year old, he was much better at occupying his time, but he didn't know that, of course.
'Just one little thing I want you to do,' Julie said.
'Not hoovering,' he thought to himself.
'I've put the washing machine on. It won't be finished before I leave, so you can hang it out to dry. It looks like a good day for drying.'
When Rob lived with his parents, it had been traditional for housewives to do their washing on a Monday and if the weather was fair, his mother would have used the old clothes prop to support the linen line that stretched the length of their back garden. If it had been raining, she would have hung up the washing around the kitchen and sitting room, making the house feel damp and smell of washing powder. 'Where's the linen line and prop?' he asked innocently.
'What?'
'I don't know where the linen line is.' He opened his hands in a gesture to indicate that it was a straightforward question.
Julie smiled. 'I'll go and set up the airer.'

Rob followed her into the garden and saw her retrieve the rotary drier from behind the shed and plonk it into the hole in the lawn. 'There you are,' she said. 'The pegs are in the basket. You'll know when the machine has finished, because it will beep and the "end" light will come on. You won't be able to open the door for about a minute. I think it's got about another forty minutes to go, so I would appreciate it if you could do that for me before you go for your walk. Keep an eye on the weather though. The forecast says a twelve per cent chance of rain.

'Okay,' he said with no great enthusiasm, just as he might have done if his mother had ever asked him to perform household chores.

After Julie left for work, he decided that he had time before hanging out the washing to play a CD. Having thoroughly enjoyed the Grover Washington album, he chose another by the same artist and sat down with a newspaper. He figured that the CD would take up at least forty minutes. In fact, it was sixty five minutes before it finished.

At that point, he went outside to check on the weather. It had clouded over and rain looked like a possibility so he left the washing for a while. The last thing he wanted was to be chastised for letting the weather spoil Julie's washing. So he made himself a coffee and sat down again to watch some television.

At a little after eleven o'clock, he rose to take another look at the weather. It looked more promising so he carried out Julie's instructions. There was no method in the way he carried out his task. He mainly took the next item from the basket and hung it in the next available space on the airer. When he picked up a pair of Julie's panties, he couldn't stop himself from holding them out and imagining his wife's wonderful buttocks being

contained within these skimpy items. He had, of course, seen Kate's briefs. Hers had seemed to be a similar size to Julie's and yet surely his wife was a couple of sizes bigger.
The next item he found in the basket was a pair of his own pants. These seem to be about three times the size of Julie's. He hung them next to his wife's and found another delightful looking pair of hers so that his briefs were now hung between two pairs of Julie's. It gave him some kind of strange pleasure to have his next to hers and he continued alternating them. There were three pairs of Julie's to two of his. He stood back and smiled. He was sure that his mother never took such simple pleasure from her Monday chore.
By eleven twenty, he had donned his shoes and was ready for his walk. He took another look at the sky and decided there was now little chance of rain so he locked the front door and ventured down his drive. He felt a strange sense of freedom.
If he followed his wife's instructions to repeat their previous walk, he would have turned right out of his drive, but as he gazed up the road in that direction, he saw a man heading towards him about thirty yards away. It occurred to Rob that this might be a neighbour who would engage him in conversation. With his current memory problems, this might present an embarrassing situation and he might have to go into all the details of his condition, so he turned left and ignored the stranger. He would still do the walk suggested by Julie but in the reverse order. He was sure that he could remember the way.
Sure enough, it all looked familiar and he soon reached the path that would take him across the pasture where they had seen the horse. Rob had always had a thing about horses ever since the day many years ago when he and his older brother Ken had wandered across a

farmer's field in search of conkers. Ken had assured Rob that the two horses were harmless, but when they galloped across to meet the two boys, Rob was not so sure. The two horses were just being friendly and curious but seeing them thundering across the field had been a little disconcerting. Rob remembered a Western film where the cowboy hero was struggling to break a frisky colt and got a bang on the head for his trouble.
The last thing Rob wanted today was another bang on the head so his attention turned to the path on the opposite side of the road. He remembered Julie telling him about the time they were chased by cows, but he couldn't see any cows. The footpath sign did not indicate its destination, but Rob decided to walk a little way to see where it led. After a short rise, he was able to see a little more of the field which was beside yet another farm. There seemed to be so many farms in this small village which he felt was a good thing and made South Luffenham more rural in his eyes. He liked the idea of living in a rural location.
Ahead of him was a tall tree. At the top of the tree was a large round shape which pricked his curiosity. As he quietly approached, he could see that the shape was a large bird. Could it be an owl? But owls were not usually seen in the middle of the day and surely would not sit in the top of a tree. It was silhouetted against the sky so that he couldn't make out any markings but he knew it was like no bird he had ever seen. His brother would know what it was because Ken had always studied the birdlife of Britain ever since he received a book on the subject as a Christmas present. Rob continued to creep forward never taking his eyes from the bird and that was why he suddenly found his right foot squelching in a cow pat. The splat and his sudden movement to move his foot was enough to cause the

bird to lift off and it was soon rising in the air with just the slightest movement of its wings.
Rob forgot about his soiled shoe as the huge bird seemed to float around in circles no longer bothered by Rob's presence below. Now he could see the markings which were a glorious mixture of brown, black and cream. It was definitely a bird of prey, but he didn't know which. He knew it wasn't a peregrine or a kestrel. Suddenly, with a few flaps of its large wings, it disappeared over the village and out of sight. Rob sighed, disappointed to see it gone and wished that he could have shared the experience with Julie. He looked down at the mess on his shoe. He wiped it as best he could on the grass and decided that it would wear off as he continued with his walk, which was still taking him up the rise.
A thunderous noise took him by surprise as a heavy freight train burst through alongside the field to his left. He hadn't realised that there was a railway in the dip below. In fact, he hadn't previously seen any signs of the railway anywhere in the village. It struck him as a little disappointing that the square-fronted locomotive that hauled the train was not hugely different from one he might have seen in the seventies. He would have expected that after forty years of development, railway engines would be sleeker and more streamlined. By now, he was at the top of the rise and could see a few buildings a little further away and guessed that these might be connected to the railway. Stations were often sited at the edge of towns and villages.
He was pleased to know that Doctor Beeching's cuts hadn't removed this particular line. King's Lynn had been badly hit. There was still a railway between Lynn and Cambridge, but those to Hunstanton, Norwich and Wisbech had all been removed. At least, that was how things stood in 1979.

He was curious to see the station and discover where this line led. He guessed as the buses ran between Stamford and Uppingham, that this railway would do the same. Julie had told him that the local bus service was circuitous and infrequent, so perhaps the trains might provide an alternative means of reaching nearby towns.
As he passed a dividing hedge, he was suddenly faced with the sight of a cow occupying the path ahead and it was staring directly at him. Beside the beast was a young calf. He remembered his wife's tale of the herd chasing them, but there were no dogs about and he was less concerned about cows than he was horses. He had crossed many a field that contained cows and never felt threatened. Bullocks and, of course, bulls might be much more of a concern, but not cows. Nevertheless, he still decided to steer a course off the recognised path to give the mother and calf plenty of room. The cow's eyes followed him all the way to the end of the field where a gate led onto another path, this time between two hedges. He gave one last look back at the cow to see she was still staring at him. He had been right. The biggest danger from cows is what they leave behind and he gave his shoe another scrape on the grass.
This new path emerged onto a road quite close to a level crossing. He looked both left and right but the road to the right seemed to head out to open countryside while to the left, there were a few more buildings and a level crossing. Some of these nearby buildings looked as though they may have been used in days gone by for storage and loading goods to the railway but that was clearly no longer the case as there was no longer a station and no railway sidings. Rob felt disappointed.

He was just about to walk over the level crossing to have a look up the road when the lights started flashing. This must be a very busy line he thought to himself. Cars and lorries soon started queuing up to cross from both sides and Rob felt a little exposed. There was no footpath and he would have to wait until the vehicles had all left before he dared walk across the line. Eventually a two carriage railcar roared through the crossing. Again, Rob didn't think its appearance was that much different from those in 1979 except that this one had an interesting livery of what he decided was magenta and light blue – or was it grey? It passed so quickly, he couldn't tell. As the train disappeared from view, he just had time to read the destination board on the rear. It read "Stansted." He'd heard the name before but couldn't quite place it. Then he remembered a "London Stansted" airport. Did that mean this train was headed for London ... and with only two carriages?

He looked at his watch. It was seven minutes to twelve. Perhaps he ought to return the way he came, but that would mean passing the protective cow again. In any case, he was curious as to what lay up the road ahead. He figured that this was still part of his village and the road would lead back in a circle so he ventured across the line where he soon came to a bridge over a stream, presumably the same unnamed stream that ran through his village, although this looked a little wider.

Crossing the stream meant in his mind, that he was now on the right side for his part of the village. What he didn't know was that this wasn't the stream that ran through South Luffenham. This was the River Chater, despite not looking much like a river at this point.

The road was now climbing up a slope and he continued, all the time seeing that there were buildings ahead although now more sparsely spaced. There was no footpath on this road and whenever vehicles passed him, he would mount the grass verge and wait until they had gone by. He was starting to regret his decision to climb this road as it was soon clear that he had left the village, and yet there were still houses ahead. A further train sped past below him. It was another railcar but headed in the opposite direction.

A further look at his watch told him that it was now twelve minutes past twelve and he should be making his way home. Julie said she would return for lunch but she hadn't quoted a time. Ahead were several houses. Surely this was the northern edge of South Luffenham so he continued thinking that he would now loop round to his road, but a sign told him that this wasn't his village. It was North Luffenham. He remembered a road about a hundred yards from their house name "North Luffenham Road." So all he had to do was find that road and it would take him back.

He followed a footpath sign which he thought might bypass North Luffenham, but it merely provided a short cut into the village. He was now in a strange village of which he knew nothing. He wished that he had studied a map of the area before he had set off, but he hadn't anticipated any problems. He knew he wasn't actually lost because if it came to it, he could always turn around and retrace his steps but that would indicate failure. No, he was determined to find a different road or path back to his village.

Then he struck lucky, because after a few more yards, he spotted a road sign pointing to South Luffenham just as there were a few spots of rain. Julie would be upset if her washing got wet, but in his anxiety to suddenly make haste, his ankle twisted on the kerb as he stepped off it to cross the road, jarring his heel into the bargain. The kerb wasn't exceptionally high and a sprightly twenty year old would have been able to

cushion the misjudged drop but Rob's joints were a little stiffer than he expected despite being quite fit for a sixty year old.
The pain shot through his heel and he had to hobble the few yards across the quiet road, where he stopped to gain his breath and take stock. He had no idea how far he still had to walk or how long it would take. Now would be a good time to use a mobile phone, but he had left his at home. It never occurred to him to bring it. There was nothing for it; he just had to hobble home as best he could. It was going to take a long time.
After ten tortuous minutes, he came to a signed public footpath, but like all the other similar signs he had seen that day, there was no indication of the destination. As the path seemed to go in the wrong direction, he was ready to ignore it and carry on, but just ahead was a bridge over the stream he had passed earlier. He paused to rest his injury and look at the stream. If he crossed it, he would be back on the wrong side again. Perhaps the stream meandered a lot and he might cross it yet again, but he wasn't sure.
Just then an elderly couple came into view. At least, they looked elderly to Rob, but were in fact, a similar age to him. From a distance, it looked to Rob like they were skiing because they were using walking poles which he had never seen before. He decided to ask them about the path.
As they came nearer, he could see that they weren't skiing; merely walking along with the ski sticks in their hands. Perhaps they were practising for a skiing holiday.
'Excuse me,' he said in his most polite voice and making sure his Norfolk accent wasn't too discernible. 'Can you tell me where this path leads to?'
'Yes,' said the man. 'It leads into North Luffenham. Is that where you want to go?'

'No, I want to go to South Luffenham,' Rob replied.
'Well, you just follow this road,' the man responded. 'You'll come to another road from your right. Just ignore that and follow the main road. Whereabouts in the village do you want to be?'
Rob couldn't remember the name of his road, but he couldn't admit that. 'I need to be this side of the stream which is why I wondered why the road crosses it here.'
'This isn't the stream in South Luffenham,' the lady said. 'This is the River Chater.'
'River?' said Rob. 'It looks like a stream to me.'
'Well, it does become a little wider as it gets nearer to Ketton,' she said.
'Of course,' Rob said remembering that Julie had told him that the stream fed into a river. Now it all made sense. 'Thank you for your help. Are you going skiing?'
They laughed. 'Don't make fun of these,' the man said. 'They've given us a new lease of life. With these we can walk a lot further than before. You should get some. They take away some of the pressure on your lower limbs and give your upper body more exercise. Perhaps you don't suffer from arthritis?'
'Well, I think I do,' Rob replied. 'And I've just twisted my ankle just walking off a kerb, would you believe. I forgot that I'm not twenty years old anymore.' He was pleased with his little private joke.'
'Well, none of us are,' the man said. 'It's not too far to South Luffenham. Enjoy your walk as best you can. We'd best be off. Goodbye.'
When he re-started, he found that the pain in his heel had practically disappeared and even the twisted ankle had eased. If only he could sit down somewhere and completely rest it, he was sure that he could make more rapid progress. At least the rain hadn't amounted to anything.

Just around the corner from the stream, he could see a railway bridge crossing above the road – another good indication that he was headed in the right direction. What he didn't like though, was walking along a road with no footpath. Fortunately, it wasn't a very busy road.
A little further on, he came to the road the man had warned him about and he was soon beyond that and feeling happier about the direction in which he was heading, but then he heard a squealing of brakes behind him. He turned to see a cloud of smoke and dust rising from beneath a red sports car. The driver had realised at the very last moment that he did not have right of way at the junction and had slammed on his brakes in a fine example of an emergency stop. He was soon on his way again in the direction of South Luffenham leaving the acrid smell of brake dust to hit Rob's senses as he hugged the roadside, there still being no footpath on which to seek refuge.
Rob felt a strange sense of déjà vu. The smell and the noise had aroused some kind of memory, but unfortunately, he couldn't remember what. He would have to ask Julie if this meant anything to her. It could be a good sign for his memory.

Meanwhile, Julie had returned from work and finding the front door locked and no sign of Rob, she guessed that he was still on his walk and must return very soon. She went out into the garden and re-arranged her washing, thinking that it had taken her many years to teach her husband how to hang washing; now she had to start all over again.
After that, she prepared a light lunch ready for his return. By twelve forty five, there was still no sign of him. She needed to get lunch out of the way as soon as

possible as she had a conference call booked with some work colleagues. She decided to call his mobile, only to hear it ringing in the sitting room. 'Aargh! What's the point of having a mobile and then leaving it at home?' she thought to herself.

She considered going to look for him, but there seemed no point. If he had managed to get lost, she wouldn't know where to look and if he was on the correct path, it was just a matter of time before he re-appeared.

She couldn't wait any longer and so she sat down to eat her lunch alone. It was only a ploughman's lunch that she had concocted based on the ingredients she had available, which was a pork pie, some cheddar cheese, pickle and tomatoes. She found a packet of crisps to make it go a little further. Rob would have the same when he eventually returned. At least it wouldn't spoil. She tucked into her own meal.

A little while later, she had finished her ploughman's and there was still no sign of her husband. Now she was starting to worry. Could he really have got himself lost? Or could he be in some sort of trouble? She ventured into the road to see if he was on his way, but there was no sign. She didn't know what to do. If she headed down the road to look for him, she might be going in the wrong direction. She decided that it was best to wait in the house. She wondered if he had any identification on him but found his wallet lying in its usual place. She supposed there was the possibility that he had suffered another loss of memory. She shouldn't have left him alone. If anything had happened, she would never be able to live with herself.

She poured a glass of water from the tap and told herself to stay calm. She picked up a newspaper for something to occupy her mind and sat down at the kitchen table.

After a few more minutes, the front door opened and Julie rushed into the sitting room just as Rob threw himself onto the settee.
‘Where have you been?’ she demanded as though he was a naughty boy who had misbehaved.
Rob threw off his shoes, forgetting about the remnants of the cow pat and lifted his injured foot onto the arm of the settee and lay on his back. ‘I went for a walk like you suggested, but I managed to twist my ankle.’
‘Where was this?’ she asked.
‘On the end of my foot,’ he replied.
‘You know what I meant,’ she said.
‘I stepped off a kerb in North Luffenham and forgot that I'm not twenty years old anymore.’ He felt his little joke deserved another airing but Julie wasn't in the mood for levity.
‘You weren't supposed to go to North Luffenham! I told you which way to go. You just had to follow the same path as last week.’
Rob resented being treated like a child. ’Well, I went a different way. I wanted to explore the area a bit more. What's the problem?’
‘The problem is I didn't know where you were and you weren't here when I got home. Why didn't you leave a note or take your bloody ‘phone with you?’
‘I didn't know I was going to twist my ankle, did I?’
‘How bad is it?’ she asked.
‘It's easing,’ he replied. ‘I just thought I'd rest it for a few minutes.’
‘Is it the same ankle that you injured a couple of years ago?’
‘How would I know?’ he asked.
She sighed. ‘Look, I can't deal with this now. I've got a conference call in a few minutes. Your lunch is on the kitchen table when you're ready.’
‘What's a conference call?’ he asked.

‘Four of us talking at the same time,’ she replied.
‘Is it HR again and are you going to get annoyed?’
‘There are two people from HR and one from my team. One of the HR chaps is very IT literate so he knows what he’s talking about so I have to be careful how I word things. He looks after all the HR requirements for things like Excel macros and mail merge.’
Rob looked at her as though she was talking a foreign language, but he knew that her talking to HR was never a good sign.
‘Never mind,’ she said. ‘We’ll talk later. You need an ice-pack on that. I’ll fetch it for you.’

After eating his lunch, Rob spent the afternoon on the settee with his foot up, reading the newspaper that he had started reading earlier and made a start on the crossword. He could hear Julie talking in the next room. He was still curious about a conference call, but, of course, he could only hear her voice and she didn’t seem to have that much to say and when she did, her voice was even and calm.
Eventually, she said ‘Right then. ‘Bye everybody ... yeah ... yeah ... ‘bye.’
She joined him in the sitting room. ‘That wasn’t so bad,’ she said. ‘Everyone seems to be happy. I’m ready for a cup of tea. How’s the ankle?’
‘I think it’s going to be all right.’ He stood up and put some weight on it. ‘Yeah, it’s not too bad. That ice-pack took down the swelling.’
‘I can think of another use for that to reduce swelling,’ she said. She was obviously now in a better mood.
‘That’s not as much fun as my preferred method,’ he said realising her jest. ‘Shall I make the tea?’ he asked.

'Yes, that seems like a good idea. Shall we sit outside and then you can tell me all about your little trip this morning.'
A few minutes later, they were, indeed, drinking tea on the patio.
'So how did you end up in North Luffenham?' she asked.
'Before I tell you that, I've got to ask if I've ever had a road accident. You see, I saw someone doing an emergency stop and the sounds and the smell gave me a feeling of déjà vu, but it was fleeting.'
'I can't think of anything in particular, but I'm not with you all the time. You might have seen something when you were commuting between Lynn and Peterborough – or any other time and not told me.'
'Oh, well,' he said. 'It was just a thought. I wondered if it was a good sign for my memory.
Anyway, I set off to do the same walk that we did last week, but I thought I'd reverse it because things often look different in another direction. But when I got to the road over the stream, I saw the path on the other side of the road and I thought I'd have a quick look. I remembered you telling me about the time we were chased by cows, so I thought I'd have a quick look and see if it triggered anything. It didn't, but I saw this great big bird of prey sitting at the top of the tree. It looked like a hawk or something – and then it took off and just floated up in the air hardly moving its wings. I wish you'd have been with me.'
'It was probably a Red Kite,' Julie said. 'They pick up the thermals. That's how they gain height so easily. Did you notice the shape of its tail?'
'Um ... not really,' he replied.
'Did it look like this,' she asked as she did something on her mobile and handed it to him.

'Yes ... yes, that's it. Is that a Red Kite? Wow! They're quite rare aren't they?'
'Not anymore. There are quite a few around here now. You might also see a buzzard or two, but their tails are a different shape and buzzards are a little smaller.'
Rob was a little disappointed that he hadn't seen something rare, but at the same time, pleased that he might see more Red Kites. 'Anyway, it flew off over the village and then I saw a goods train thundering through the little dip and I thought there might be a station just over the rise so I went to explore that, not realising there were cows the other side of the hedge – and some calves. But I made it across the field without being chased. Of course, there wasn't a station, but I saw the stream and it looked like the road would just lead back into the village. After a while, I realised my mistake but I was soon in North Luffenham; which is where I twisted my ankle. That slowed me up. I saw the road to South Luffenham and followed that. That may have been a bit longer than our walk the other day, but I got to see something different.'
Julie shook her head. 'You might have got lost. You should have listened to me. I wouldn't have thought it very nice walking along the road.'
'No, that's true, but it's over now. Oh, and I saw these two elderly people walking along with ski sticks in their hands. Why would they do that?'
Julie looked at him for a moment wondering what he meant. 'Oh, I expect they were walking poles. A lot of people use them these days. We tried some but gave up on them. Anyway, I'm supposed to be working. I have to write up some notes about that meeting. I'd better get on with it.' She gave him a little peck on the forehead.

Chapter 15

Julie was not feeling optimistic that their trip to the hospital would result in any great change in Rob's condition, so she felt that it still fell to her to make the effort to try to restore his memory. Although, the photograph albums had already been unsuccessful, she thought that perhaps the more recent digital images might be more fruitful, so one evening she insisted that they sat down together in front of a computer screen to look at some more.

Apart from hoping to jog his memory, she also wanted to drag him away from the television which was occupying more and more of his time, so much so that she decided that she might scream at him if he watched one more episode of *Hi-de-Hi!* or '*Allo Allo*' as much as she had enjoyed them herself when they were first aired.

When Rob had first moved to a digital camera, he liked to download his photographs to their computer, as his first such device did not have a huge memory unlike his present camera which used a sixty four gigabyte memory card. Rob, being very methodical, had set up separate folders to make it easy to find his images when required. This was his domain. Julie was used to a laptop for work and seldom used the home computer. Rob, however, didn't like laptops. He preferred a solid keyboard and mouse with a proper monitor screen.

Since his accident, he had tried to use the computer a few times, but he was still struggling, so it was left to Julie to guide him towards a folder called *Pictures* where lay all the sub-folders that had been created by Rob as and when required. His eyes lit upon one entitled *Lake District.*

'I've been to The Lake District,' he said.

'Of course you have,' Julie replied. 'You took these photographs.'
'No, I went last year ... um, 1978, I mean. I went with a couple of friends. We went camping in Newlands. Eddy had borrowed his father's Mark IV Cortina, so we headed over to a little place called Little Town. He'd found it on a map and thought it wouldn't be as crowded as the big towns like Windermere and Keswick. He was right. We didn't see anyone. It wasn't a town at all.'
'I'm not surprised that you didn't see anyone,' said Julie. 'I wouldn't even call it a village. There's not much more than a few farm buildings.' She had heard this story before but choose to humour him.
'We only stayed two nights,' he continued. 'The first night was all right as we settled in after our long drive. The next day we started climbing up the side of a mountain, but we didn't really know where we were going. We had a map, but it was the wrong scale and we got into trouble. We hadn't bothered taking a drink so after an hour or so, feeling thirsty, we decided to retrace our steps but it all looked different going back.'
'I know,' said Julie, 'and you eventually found someone to guide you and you did make it back. You then drove into Portinscale to get some food and drink, but went home the next day after it rained all night and the tent let in water.'
'Oh, you've heard the story before,' Rob said. 'Of course you have. Let's have a look at these photographs.' He felt a little silly. Naturally, she would know all about such boring stories and now he was being boring all over again.
She opened the Lake District folder and they started looking at the pictures. Rob was amazed at the sharpness and the rich colours of the images compared to his old snaps and said so.

‘That was last year,’ Julie said. ‘The weather wasn’t always too brilliant, but on the days when the sun shone, it was glorious. We can’t manage the big fells anymore, despite going to the gym regularly. You can’t really train for steep hills in a gym. In any case, it’s not always necessary to reach the tops if you want to see some lovely scenery.’ She went quiet to see if the photographs caused any reaction with Rob. He remarked how lovely it all looked but it didn’t stir any memories.
‘Let’s try Switzerland,’ Julie said. ‘The problem with The Lake District is that when we’re there, we spend most of the time just the two of us. There’s little chance to socialise ... which is all right when you’re seeking solitude around the Fells as we do. In Switzerland, we were on a package holiday and made very good friends with Andy and Shirley. They shared the same table as us in the hotel.’ She opened the Switzerland folder.
‘I can’t believe that we’ve been to Switzerland,’ he said. ‘That would always have been one of my dream holidays. Was it good?’
‘It was wonderful,’ she replied.
‘How did we afford it? I always thought of it as being very expensive.’
‘It is,’ she said, ‘but we went by coach and made sure that a lot of the meals were included in the price.’
‘How long does it take to get there by coach?’ he asked.
‘On this occasion, we stayed overnight in Belgium ... and then we reached our hotel in time for the evening meal the next day. It’s a bit of a slog but the coaches are very comfortable and they stop a few times so that we can stretch our legs. I don’t like flying and you don’t like airports. We’ve been talking about taking a train if we go again. Eurostar is very good these days.’
‘What’s Eurostar?’ he asked.

'The train that goes from London through the tunnel to Paris or Brussels direct. For us, it's harder to actually get to London but we know people who have used Eurostar and they say they would do it again.'
'So they finally built a tunnel, did they? This place looks nice,' he said pointing at the screen.
'That's Gruyeres,' she said. 'It's one of our favourite places. It's where the cheese is made.'
'Which cheese?' he asked.
'Gruyeres, of course,' she said.
'I've never heard of it,' he said.
She sighed. 'You young twenty year olds ... you know nothing. Everyone's heard of Gruyeres cheese. The cheese factory is in the newer part of the town and these pictures are of the old medieval area which is built on a hill. It's surrounded by a wall and there is a castle at one end. There ... that's us eating pasta in a roadside cafe,' she said as they moved on to another delightful scene. 'I thought we had a photo of Shirley, but I don't see it,' she said as she quickly ran through each of the Gruyeres images. 'It wasn't a very good one. I expect you've deleted it. You're always deleting stuff to save on space.'
'Do we have to worry about space?' he asked.
'Not these days,' she replied. 'We used to when we first had a PC, but nowadays we've got hundreds of gigabytes.'
Rob didn't know what a gigabyte was and decided not to ask. 'I don't see many mountains in these photographs. I thought Switzerland was all mountains.'
'We saw plenty of mountains and there are some around Gruyeres but not necessarily snow-capped. There'll be some higher ones in the later photographs but Gruyeres is hilly rather than mountainous.' She moved on to the next town. 'Here, this is Interlaken.

That's surrounded by mountains. Interlaken is German for "between the lakes."
'Do you speak German?' he asked.
'No, I just know that's what it means.'
'How did we get on with the locals if we don't speak the language?'
'Nearly everyone in Switzerland speaks English – at least in the leisure and hospitality services. Interlaken is an important centre for travel in the Bernese Oberland. We stopped there on the way towards Grindelwald which we'll see in a moment.' She realised that she was sounding like a travel agent trying to sell the holiday to Rob.
'It looks nice,' said Rob. 'I just wish I could remember going there. I've always wanted to go to Switzerland – and now that I have, I don't remember it.' His shoulders slumped.
Julie moved the pictures on to Grindelwald. 'This is way up in the mountains,' she said. 'In Grindelwald, we caught a cable car ... well, gondola, actually. We could only go halfway as it was getting too windy further up, but we still got some lovely views of The Eiger and The Jungfrau. There's a railway that goes right to the top of The Jungfrau. It tunnels through the mountain, but we didn't have time to do that. That's the problem with a coach holiday. You only get a few hours in each location.'
Rob was transfixed by the images, but still there was no sign of recognition. Julie was feeling frustrated at the lack of progress in her quest so she skipped a few photos until she reached one of four people sipping coffee at a lakeside restaurant. 'That's Andy and Shirley,' she said. 'Are you sure they don't look familiar? We became very good friends. You told me that you loved Shirley's laugh and you spent the week

trying to amuse her whenever you could. I wasn't sure whether you fancied her or not.'
'She looks about seventy,' Rob said. 'Why would I fancy her ... especially when I've got you? No, I don't recognise them. Where is this anyway?'
'It's Lucerne ... where the famous covered bridge is. We had good intentions to keep in touch with them after the holiday because we got on so well, but after a couple of e-mails and some shared photographs, it all lapsed.' She skipped a few more pictures to show him the covered bridge. 'We loved Lucerne. It was our last day before we headed home.' She closed the folder and sighed.
Rob asked 'You said I didn't like airports. Does that mean that I've been in a plane?'
'Yes. You don't remember our weekend in Venice? It was out of season when it wasn't too crowded. The weather wasn't brilliant but, in a way, that made it seem more atmospheric, especially with fewer people around ... but you hated all the waiting around in the airport and I dreaded the flight home.'
'So, how often do we go abroad?' he asked.
'Not as often as most people, but we've been to Austria and Bruges. We've been to Switzerland twice. The first time was about 2002 when the children were old enough to appreciate it. That was a coach holiday as well. That was in the French speaking side of the country so we had a day in Chamonix. We wanted to go in a cable car up Mont Blanc, but the queue was too long so we went up in one the other side of the valley and had great views of Mont Blanc. That was lovely. I wish you could remember.'
'So do I,' he said. 'Do we have any photos of the other Swiss holiday?'

'Yes, but they're in an album somewhere in the loft and they're not as good as these.' She let out another sigh. 'This isn't working is it?'
'No, but I'm enjoying it. Can I look at some more? I see there's a folder entitled *Norfolk.* Did we really go to Norfolk for a holiday?'
'Yes, we went just last year,' she replied. 'We still go over to Norfolk quite frequently but it's just a bit too far to go there and back and see everything in a day so we sometimes stop over for a couple of nights. This time, we rented a small cottage in Castle Acre. It gave us chance to see parts of Norfolk we hadn't seen before. Switzerland was wonderful, but I sometimes think we enjoy Norfolk just as much. It's very relaxing.'
'I find that all hard to believe,' he said, '... holidaying in Norfolk when we used to live there, I mean.' He opened up the Norfolk folder.
'I'll leave you to it,' Julie said. 'You take your time looking at these. You know what to do with them now. When you've finished, just click on the little cross in the corner to close things down.'
Rob spent the next hour perusing all the images that he could find, but still nothing restored his missing memories even though he recognised a few of the scenes from his limited travels during the sixties and seventies. Many of the scenes from Norfolk were familiar to him but not all. He was surprised to see a few of King's Lynn that demonstrated big changes since 1979. A view of the historic Customs House showed that a lot of work had been carried out to make the area more attractive. The unsavoury muddy Purfleet of his time was now an attractive lagoon. At last, he thought, the council had actually made improvements to the area. He recalled the critical remarks his parents had made when Broad Street and New Conduit Street were modernised in the sixties,

although he barely remembered those streets before the unpopular changes. Nor did he remember the many buildings that were pulled down in the cause of modernisation. He decided that he must pay another visit to Lynn to see the latest changes for himself.

Julie slumped down on the settee. Nothing she had tried seemed to help Rob's condition. The doctors seemed confident that his was not a physical problem so what had caused it? And what was special about losing forty years of memories? Why not thirty? Or fifty? Something must have happened forty years ago. She often wondered if it had something to do with that Kate person; but what? She considered questioning him about her, but she knew that just mentioning her name seemed to really upset him so she decided to avoid that particular subject.

She wondered how long this was all going to last. Could it be that he would never regain his memory? That would be problematic in so many ways. She didn't believe that in his current state of mind that he actually loved her. He'd already proved that he was attracted to her but love would take a little longer if, indeed, it ever happened. Nevertheless, she was sure their marriage would survive, but what about their finances? He couldn't return to his current employment without repeating his training and because he wasn't actually unfit to work, she suspected that he might struggle to claim benefits.

In 1979, he wasn't fully trained as a surveyor so he couldn't easily return to that. In any case, she was sure that no one would employ a sixty year-old trainee surveyor. If this continued for just a few more weeks, they could probably manage financially, but beyond that, they would be back to the old days of struggling to make ends meet. She wasn't sure if she could face that again.

When Rob re-appeared from looking at the photographs, she asked 'Anything?'

He shook his head. 'No, but I enjoyed trying,' he said. 'There didn't seem to be many people in those photographs ... apart from that group at Lucerne.'

'No, we've tried including ourselves in some of the views, but we just seem to spoil them. Who wants to see middle-aged people wearing dirty old walking boots and waterproofs spoiling a lovely view of the likes of Newlands or the Langdale Pikes? We still haven't invested in a selfie-stick.'

'What's that when it's at home?' he asked.

'A selfie-stick is a thin rod that you can attach to a mobile phone so that you can operate the camera at arm's length allowing you to take a picture of yourself. When you go abroad, you see all these tourists doing it. They have to prove to someone that they've been to these places ... and then they post them on-line. I've heard of people who go to see the Taj Mahal to get a photo of themselves standing in front of it and don't even bother to look at the building. What's the point of that?'

'It does seem crazy,' he said. 'In my day, I used a rubber bulb to operate the button to take a photograph remotely. Or you could use a self-timer.'

'Gosh, I'd forgotten about the old bulb mechanism,' Julie said. 'Most of the time, it didn't work. Young people would think we're daft if we tried that now.'

'Anyway,' Rob added,' I'd like to have seen some photos of you.'

'Why?'

'Because you're nice to look at,' he replied.

‘That’s the nicest thing you’ve said to me in years,’ she said.
‘Well, I’m sorry to hear that. I can’t say I know that many middle-aged women, but you’re very attractive.’ He nearly added ‘for your age,’ but he stopped himself. ‘I know it sounds like a funny thing to say after thirty odd years of marriage, but I am growing very fond of you.’
She smiled. She knew he found her body attractive. His constant interest in sex was testament to that, but this latest comment showed signs that if he didn’t recover his memory, there was a good chance of him finding love. ‘Are you sure it’s not just my body that you’re growing fond of?’
‘That as well,’ he said as she thrust her bosom in his direction. ‘Oh, hello, boys. Are you coming out to play?’
‘It’s as I thought,’ she said. ‘It’s my body you’re after.’
He pulled her closer and felt her impressive breasts against his own chest. ‘That’s true, but there is more.’
‘And what’s that?’ she asked, this time pushing her crotch in his direction.
His hands started wandering and his lips found hers. He didn’t answer her.
‘Well?’ she asked.
‘Can I come back to that later? I’ve got other things on my mind at the moment.’
She was aware of his member stirring in his underpants and he reached down to make himself more comfortable.
‘At least we don’t have to rely on Viagra like some couples of our age,’ she said.
‘What’s that?’ he asked.
‘It’s a magic pill used by people who can’t get it up,’ she replied.
‘It all sounds a bit like *A Brave New World.* Do they have happiness pills as well?’

'Some people like to take such things, but believe me, there is a price to pay ... and I don't mean in money. Anyway, before you get carried away, I'm not doing it on the floor again. We've done all our experimentation when we were much younger. We know – or rather, I know - what works best for us and at the moment, I'd rather have a cup of hot chocolate before we go to bed.'

As they sat down to drink their hot chocolate, Julie said 'Your problem started with a bang on the head. I thought I might try giving you a little tap on the head ... and if that doesn't work, I'll make it a little bit harder each time until it works. What do you think?'
He knew she was joking. 'I wish it was as easy as that. I know this isn't much fun for you, but if it's any consolation, I am enjoying getting to know you. It's a bit like dating a new girlfriend, except that I've already won you so there isn't the same pressure to succeed.'
She gave him one of her stern looks. 'Don't think I'm always going to be a pushover. I'm being nice to you at present just to restore your memory.'

Chapter 16

During the next few days, Rob learned, with much help from Julie, more and more about this new modern world. He found that there was still no cure for the common cold; that most forms of cancer could be treated if discovered early enough, yet some were still death sentences despite the billions spent on research. He learned from Julie of the many wars that had been waged since 1979, some of which still raged, although she admitted that she didn't always understand why many of the conflicts had arisen.

The cold war with the Soviet Union was long finished, but relationships with Russia, China, Iran and North Korea were not good and that fresh conflict could erupt at any time, given that each of these nations were ruled by undemocratic leaders who like to exert their power from time to time.

Many countries had ceased to exist, such as Yugoslavia and Czechoslovakia, to be replaced by their constituent nations. Other countries had changed their name making it hard for the average person to keep abreast of them.

Rob still didn't understand Brexit and the ongoing arguments. For instance, if the country was leaving the EU, why did we still have to negotiate the terms on which we left? If you hand in your notice to your employer, you don't spend years negotiating the terms of your leaving. You serve your notice period and go. Julie said it was because so many people in Britain still wanted to remain and were resisting the move.

He also learnt with Julie's assistance, about e-mails. To him, this seemed liked a modern and more personalised version of the facsimile machines (or fax)

that his company had used to communicate with other organisations. He perused his various e-mail communications, but the names of the correspondents meant nothing to him.
None of this helped to restore his memory and he began placing a huge amount of hope upon his upcoming hospital visit, because he still didn't feel that he was at home. To him, home was King's Lynn with his parents and friends, and most of all, with Kate. He was in a strange world with a strange family, as lovely as they were. He wasn't sixty years old. He was twenty, with his life before him, not lost to hidden memories.
However, he was growing ever fond of Julie and fully understood why he might have fallen in love with her all those years ago, but he wasn't there yet. He knew that when he did eventually regain his memory, Kate would be consigned to his past and that saddened him, but this would be compensated by his love for Julie and his new family.
She had used the on-line Yellow Pages to discover that there were several hypnotherapists in the area, but before she took any action about this, they would see what the doctor had to say.
Jed paid him another visit, but, if anything, it was even less successful than his previous call as they both still felt like strangers to each other. While the two men sat on the patio drinking coffee, Jed saw a bumble bee searching for pollen among the lavender stems. He asked 'Do you know which is the most dangerous bee?'
'No, I don't think I do,' Rob replied.
'Hepatitis B,' Jed said.
Rob had never heard of Hepatitis B, as it wasn't so prevalent in the 1970s and therefore, he didn't laugh. Jed didn't bother with any further attempts at humour and dearly wished for his old friend back, for his efforts

to revive memories fell on the same stony ground as his jokes.

Julie had trusted Rob to stay at home on his own more frequently, knowing that she ought to spend more time in the office, especially as she had to take a day's leave for the hospital visit on Friday. At first, he was quite happy with his own company, but after a while, he wanted to get out and about. Seeing his car in the drive just made him feel more frustrated. The Skoda looked more inviting than his old Datsun. In 1979, he would never have thought that a Skoda could look more impressive than a Datsun. How times had changed. He sometimes sat in his car, fiddling with the controls, trying to familiarise himself ready for the day when he could start the engine and head off into the wild blue yonder of Rutland – or preferably, back to Norfolk. No one would know if he just started it up and went for a short spin, but he guessed that his insurance policy might be invalidated by driving against medical instructions. Not only that, but the six-speed gearbox bothered him a little. His Datsun had the usual four gears. And so he waited until Friday came around. It couldn't come soon enough.

The Ambulatory Care Unit in the hospital was very busy. Rob realised that the unusual name was a pseudonym for *Outpatients.* He couldn't understand why the name had been changed from his day, especially to such a meaningless title. Who used the word *ambulatory?* After announcing his arrival to one of the two receptionists, he and Julie managed to find seats, but they had to sit apart for about ten minutes until they were able to swap their places when another couple moved.

There seemed to be lots of activity from nurses and orderlies and some other employees in civilian attire who seemed to walk around with pieces of paper in their hands, but there were no signs of anyone who might be construed as a doctor. If all these people waiting, were expecting to see a doctor, it was going to be a very long wait. After the apparent efficiency of the Uppingham Surgery, he wondered why the hospital couldn't operate a similar system of appointments. He overheard someone say she had been there since nine o'clock and still hadn't seen anyone. It was now ten thirty five.

He heard his name called out and felt hopeful that he might jump the big queue. 'Mr Lennard? Robert Lennard?'

He jumped up with his paperwork in his hand. 'I just need to check your blood pressure,' the young nurse announced. She led him into a small room down the corridor while Julie kept their seats. As the nurse closed the door, she was still looking at some notes. 'So you had a blow to the head. We don't need any blood tests,' she said. 'When did you last have your dressing changed?'

'It was Monday morning,' he replied.

'Oh, we'd better change it and hope the doctor doesn't want to see the wound,' she said. 'How have you been?'

'I've been fine, but I still haven't regained my memory.'

'Your memory? What do you mean?' she asked.

'I woke up from my accident thinking it was 1979,' he said, feeling a little annoyed that she wasn't aware of that fact.

'How weird,' she said. 'I've never heard of such a thing. Is it getting any better?'

'No, not really,' he said. 'I was hoping I might get some answers today.'

'Let's hope so,' said the nurse. 'The doctors are still doing the wards at the moment, but we'll get someone to talk to you as soon as we can. She removed Rob's dressing and said 'That's healed up nicely. I don't think we need to replace that. Let's do your blood pressure and your temperature.'
Five minutes later, he was back in the waiting room telling Julie what the nurse had said about the doctors still doing the wards. Julie was not pleased but was able to occupy herself with something on her phone like many of the other people waiting. She had warned Rob to bring his Kindle and now he was glad of her advice.
Eventually, after what seemed like another hour, but was really only half that time, doctors started to appear and summon various patients. Rob didn't know if they were being seen in some kind of sequence of appointment or appearance, but the lady who had said she'd been there since nine o'clock was still there and looking more and more frustrated. Rob decided that she must be ahead of him so he concentrated on his Kindle. He was reading *Master and Commander* and was really getting into it. He was therefore almost disappointed when a young doctor called his name.
Julie insisted on joining them in the consulting room. Rob didn't recognise the doctor as being one of the ones who had already seen him on the ward and was surprised that he didn't seem to be wearing any kind of uniform. In fact, he wondered if he was actually a doctor, but he introduced himself as Doctor Waller, while appearing to study Rob's notes.
After a minute or two, he said 'Hmmm ... let's have a look at your head wound. Yes, that's healed up nicely. When was this incurred?'
'It will be two weeks on Sunday,' said Julie as Rob hesitated.

'And you were unconscious for about three days. Any headaches?'
'In the first couple of days, but none since,' replied Rob.
'Any dizziness or nausea?'
'No.'
'Any problems with your vision?'
'No ... once I got used to my varifocals.'
'Well, it's all looking good,' the doctor said. 'I think you can resume all normal activity.'
'Does that mean I can drive?' Rob asked.
'Oh, yes. I think we can discharge you. We won't need to see you again. If you have any problems, see your GP, but I don't think you will.'
'What about his memory?' asked Julie rather forcibly.
'Is that no better?' the doctor asked.
'No,' replied Rob. 'I still don't remember anything since 1979.'
'Yes, that is strange,' said the doctor. 'I think you've suffered some kind of trauma, but I would have thought by now, you should be seeing signs of recovery. This hasn't ever happened to you before has it?'
'Not that I know of,' Rob replied.
'Of course not,' said Julie, feeling aggrieved at the doctor's almost casual attitude. 'Isn't there anything you can do? What about hypnotherapy?'
'That's not something we do here. You can ask your GP if there is anyone he can refer you to, but you might have to go private, I'm afraid.'
With that, Julie made to move. 'Come on Rob. Thank you for time, Doctor.'
Rob wasn't sure if she was being sarcastic or not, but he repeated the thanks and followed her like a puppy.
As they headed back to the car, Rob wanted to calm Julie. He could tell that she was not happy that the doctor did not offer any help with his memory loss. 'I'd have thought in the twenty first century, someone might

have invented a pill that could restore my memory,' he said.
That didn't seem to help. 'At least we don't have to go back there again,' he added.
Julie glared at him. 'No, but now we've got to try and get some help from our GP. Don't hold your breath with that!'
As they neared Julie's car, Rob said 'As I can drive now, shall I take us home?'
'No, I don't like it when you drive my car. I have trouble getting the seats and the mirrors back the way I want them. You can have a drive in your car. Perhaps we'll go somewhere this afternoon. I'm hungry. Shall we go and get some lunch at the supermarket? I don't want to be bothered with preparing food when we get home.'

Rob was again amazed at the size of the superstore and was equally surprised that a supermarket would contain a cafe, although he really ought not to be surprised at anything he encountered in the twenty-first century.
It was twenty five minutes past eleven when they entered. Julie said 'They change the menu at eleven thirty. We need to hang around for a few minutes and then we can order from the lunch menu,' but then she saw that a queue had already formed and guessed that by the time they were served, the clock would have clicked around sufficiently, although this meant that the menu was not yet available for them to inspect.
'You usually have the breakfast, 'she said. 'Although you sometimes have a pie if they've got one. Let's pick up a cold drink and get in the queue.'
Twenty five minutes later, they were both tucking into their lunches and Rob asked between mouthfuls

'Where are we going this afternoon?' He was still dependent upon his wife to make all the decisions.
'Best not to go too far on a Friday. The roads will be busy everywhere and you're not going to be used to your car, so I thought we might go to Rutland Water. We'll do the peninsular. We haven't done that for a while and we can park there for free ... as long as we can find a space in the village.'
The word *peninsular* intrigued him and his spirits rose at the prospect of seeing it.
'When we've finished this,' Julie said, attending to the last few remnants of food on her plate, 'I'll give Ben a call and see if we can pay them a visit tomorrow. I think the forecast is quite good – and we can go up to the coast on the way. We'll see if that triggers any memories.'
'Remind me where they live?' he asked.
'North Wootton. It's not far from where we lived so we'll drive down our old road to see if that rings a bell with you – as well as seeing your other grandchild. Hang on, it's ringing.'
When she had finished talking to Ben, she told Rob of their plans for Saturday. 'They're going to be busy in the morning, so I think we should drive up to the coast first. How well do you remember that area?'
'Well, I know Heacham, Hunstanton, Brancaster ... I've been to Cromer as well.'
She thought for a moment. 'There's no point in going to places that you're already familiar with, but equally, we don't want to be driving too far if we have to get back to Wootton. Do you know Thornham?'
'I don't think I do,' he replied.
'Right, here's what we'll do. It'll take about two hours to drive there so we can get a drink and a comfort break at Thornham and then have a little wander along the coast path. We may be able to get a bus back to

Thornham and by then it will be time to see Ben and the children. I'll print off a bus timetable so that we can time it accordingly. I'll also check the tides ... not that it will make any difference to our arrangements. We had a lovely time last year when we did more or less the same little walk. We saw an avocet and lots of egrets.'
'What's an egret?' he asked. 'Is that a baby eagle? Surely not at the seaside?'
She laughed and the elderly couple on the next table stared across at her. 'Well, it is a bird, but it's a type of heron. They used to be quite rare but there seem to be lots of them on the coast these days.'
Rob didn't like being laughed at and went quiet until it was ready for them to leave.

The first thing that Julie did when they got home was to phone the GP's surgery. Announcing to Rob that she was third in the queue, she instructed him to make a cup of tea while she waited. He did as he was told.
Eventually, her call was answered and the lady to whom she talked gave her the expected impression that hypnotherapy was not something that they provided, but Julie explained what the Hospital doctor had told them and that they should talk to their GP. The lady on the 'phone told Julie that she would arrange for their doctor to call Rob on Monday when she was next available. She wouldn't give an exact time but thought that it would probably be in the morning and she was sure the doctor would want to talk to Rob himself unless Julie felt he was unable to handle the call.
'He's lost his memory, not his mind!' Julie said rather more abruptly than she meant.
'I'm not very optimistic about this,' she said to Rob when she had finished the call. 'I think we may have to go private, but it will be worth it if they can help.'

As Rob carefully pulled out of their drive, Julie said 'Now remember that this is a diesel car so when you fill up at the petrol station, make sure you use the black nozzle. My car is petrol, so that needs a green nozzle. Don't get them wrong. The wrong fuel can be disastrous. Now turn right up the next road.'
Rob was getting used to receiving instructions. It niggled him, but it was to be expected. He could hear Julie sucking in her breath as he struggled with the gears. He had always found four gears to be perfectly adequate. Why did he need six? And why on Earth had he bought a diesel motor. Weren't diesels for vans and lorries? 'It seemed the sensible option at the time,' Julie told him when he mentioned it. 'But time has proved us wrong. It does give us between fifty and sixty miles to the gallon, but they are not the best option if you're only doing short runs. You told me that it's important to do a long journey every now and then, so I thought it might be a good idea to take your car to Norfolk tomorrow – once you get used to driving it again.'
Despite his misgivings about driving both a Skoda and a diesel, he found this vehicle more solid and responsive than his old Datsun, but, of course, he didn't know what other modern cars felt like.

He enjoyed walking around the peninsular and admired the ever changing scenery. He didn't remember ever doing anything like this in Norfolk, but the constant threat of being mown down by passing cyclists took away some of the pleasure. Nobody seemed to bother with ringing a bell. Occasionally one of the cyclists would shout a friendly warning and some thanked them for stepping aside, but many seemed to ride past as

though pedestrians were an unnecessary inconvenience.
However, the last mile of the walk seemed to take an eternity and Rob's knees were aching so much that it was a great relief when they eventually reached his motor. So this was how it felt to be sixty years old. What made it feel worse for him was the knowledge that these aches would probably increase as he aged still further; and he didn't have the consolatory memories of the last forty years when he would have been more able to take such distances literally in his stride.
At least, the short drive home re-assured them both that he was perfectly capable of driving them both to his home county of Norfolk and he was already eagerly anticipating those old familiar haunts on the way to the less familiar village of Thornham.

Chapter 17

Rob had spent a troubled night, waking up several times after disturbing dreams. Many times over the last two weeks, he had woken fearing that he was back in a hospital and now even older than sixty.
But now that he was fully awake, he felt excited at the prospect of seeing Norfolk again, although in his mind, it had only been two weeks since he had been there. He wondered what changes he would see. He was also enthusiastic about driving his motor, ever since Julie had pointed out that although it was a diesel, it was a turbo diesel which would be so much faster than his old Datsun. His journey to Rutland Water hadn't given him any opportunity to put his foot down. In any case, on that occasion, he had been busy familiarising himself with the controls, but now he had the sporting instincts of a twenty year old to test himself and his vehicle.

As soon as they reached the A47, he was crashing through the gears and attempting an overtaking manoeuvre that the sixty year old Rob would never consider.
'Rob! For Heaven's sake! Are you trying to get us killed? This is the A47. As soon as you overtake one lorry, there'll be another just around the corner. You won't get there any quicker by driving like a lunatic. God knows there are enough idiots on the road without you swelling their ranks.'
This was how Rob usually drove in 1979 except that this vehicle had a little more overtaking power than his previous cars. He was a little surprised that Julie of all people would be a little nervous of speed, but he duly moderated his driving, especially as she was correct about there being another lorry around the next bend.

As he pulled onto the dual carriageway that served as the Castor bypass, he was sorely tempted to speed up but he was appalled at the state of the road which badly needed a fresh surface dressing and the firm suspension of the Skoda made driving at speed decidedly uncomfortable.
He commented on the surface and Julie replied 'This is nothing. You'll see a lot worse than this by the end of the day. The councils seem to act as though it's cheaper to pay compensation to motorists for damaged suspension than it is to actually repair the roads.'
Just then, an Audi SUV stormed past. 'What is the speed limit these days?' Rob asked as he suddenly realised that it might have changed since 1979.
'It's seventy on dual carriageways and motorways, and sixty on other roads,' she replied.
'Well, that woman must have been doing about ninety,' he said. 'And you thought I was driving too fast.'
As the dual carriageway came to an end, the traffic started accumulating and their progress slowed considerably. 'It's started early,' Julie said. 'It's always like this on a summer weekend, which is why I wanted us to get off to an early start.'
'I can't help my bowels,' he said.
'I know. It's not your fault,' she replied. 'I just hate this journey. It will be better once we get past Lynn and we can go round the country roads to avoid all the sheep who head for Hunstanton.' By *sheep*, she meant all the other holiday makers. In her eyes, she was not one of them.
Her original estimate of the journey taking two hours was way off. There was a slow queue at the Guyhirn roundabout, an even longer one outside of Wisbech and several around King's Lynn, but eventually, they were free of the bulk of the traffic. The route Julie had chosen was via Docking and in terms of distance was

further than the conventional way, but it was far less stressful for them both. However, they arrived at their destination feeling in desperate need of a comfort stop.
A cafe on the main coast road provided the opportunity for them both to address their needs. Rob still hadn't used his debit card for payment, so she offered to order their refreshments while he attended to something more urgent. He could have paid by cash using some of the extra that she had given him before they had left, but she had told him that it was for the bus fares when they returned from their walk. It would be easier for him to carry his wallet on the walk than for her to take her purse.
A few minutes later, they were each eagerly devouring a bacon sandwich, washed down by a mug of coffee. 'We'll do more or less the same walk we did last year,' Julie said between mouthfuls. 'It would be nice to do something a little different, but I'm hoping you will remember something by repeating it. We'll move the car into the village, but not too far, because we'll catch the bus back and that only stops on the main road.'
Rob just nodded. He had no say in the matter but would be pleased to be out of the car for a couple of hours. All along the road between Peterborough and King's Lynn, Julie had asked him if the road was familiar as he had travelled it numerous times when working at the Call Centre, but the answer was always negative. He did remember travelling between Lynn and Wisbech when he was younger, but that road had changed considerably in recent years as several villages were now bypassed, as was Wisbech itself and to him, he could have been anywhere and it wasn't until they reached the King's Lynn bypass that he recognised anything. He had often played football at some of those villages such as Tilney and Terrington, but he wasn't

sorry to have avoided all those twisty roads in the vicinity.

'I'll take the rucksack as you've got your camera,' Julie said. She checked the contents – a drink; some biscuits for a snack; sunscreen; hand-wipes and a small rug to sit upon when they stopped for a snack. She had insisted on Rob taking his own camera because that was what he usually did on a walk of this nature. She could have taken photographs with her own phone camera, but Rob had always favoured the SLR as he preferred the use of a viewfinder to an LED screen.

He strung the camera around his neck. He had practised with it in the days before this trip, but he still wasn't sure how to get the best out of it. Back in 1979, he had purchased his first SLR having spent a few months reading photographic magazines to decide on which camera best suited his budget and his needs. He had settled upon a Cosina, described as one of the best budget cameras on the market and it had the advantage of using the Pentax 'K' mount which gave him a good choice of lenses if he decided to upgrade from the Cosinon standard lens that was included with the camera. This was a 50mm fixed length lens. A Praktica camera may have been cheaper and sturdier, but that was Russian and against his principles while the Cold War still raged. A few weeks later, he had added a Miranda 135mm telephoto lens which he found gave great close ups of flowers and people. Although lacking the flexibility of a zoom lens, he understood that the quality for a fixed length lens would be higher despite the low price. At that time, he had ambitions to add an 80-200 mm zoom lens when his finances allowed it.

The weight of the DSLR around his neck was a little greater than his old Cosina. There were other differences between the two devices. The primary one was the lack of film in the new camera. It was in his nature to still be conservative with the number of images he would take. He'd sent too many films off for processing only to be disappointed when less than half of the returned snaps were satisfactory. He also felt it wrong to allow the camera to do all his thinking for him. His old camera had a metering mechanism, but this merely provided him with the information to set the aperture and the shutter speed. This may have been a nuisance but it did give him a good understanding of how to get the best results. The new one would allow him the option of doing all this if he choose, but then why fiddle about when he could just point and shoot? The same applied to focusing. It was all done for him, but at least he had the knowledge instilled in him from previously having to make decisions, unlike those people who took photographs with their 'phones and just clicked. Such people knew nothing about *depth of field* and *soft focusing*.
Before they set off, Julie insisted that Rob should apply some sun screen to his forehead and nose, as well as the bald patch on the top of his head. 'You don't want your wound to get burned,' she said. He'd never bothered much about sun protection. Even in the hot summer of 1976, he had often ventured out unprotected, but Julie wasn't prepared for either of them to take unnecessary risks.
Rob double checked all the locks on his car. He didn't trust this fancy remote locking facility. As they walked along, he wondered if he should reach out to hold Julie's hand. He would certainly have done so with Kate, but did people of their age still hold hands? He couldn't remember ever seeing his parents doing it. He

decided against it. He considered there were two types of married couples who held hands – young newly-weds or Darby and Joan couples in their twilight years and Rob and Julie were neither, although he still felt a little like a newly-wed. In any case, if Julie wanted to hold hands, he was sure that she would take the initiative, but her hands were too busy gripping the straps of the rucksack.

Thornham didn't look like a typical seaside village. For one thing, he couldn't see the sea and he wondered how far they were going to walk, but a sign indicating the coastal path reassured him a little.

The first part of their walk took them past some nice cottages built in the local materials of flint and stone.

'That's a nice place,' Julie said. 'I bet that's worth a bob or two. What do you reckon - about half a million?'

'Good Heavens!' Rob replied. 'Do you think so? It's not that big.' But, of course, Rob had no idea of the current value of property. 'If that's half a million, what's ours worth?'

'Well, it's never been valued since we moved in, but based on what other properties are going for in the village, I would say between three hundred and fifty thousand and three seventy five. Thornham is probably an expensive place to live: anywhere along this coast is.'

'We live in a house worth up to three hundred and seventy five thousand?' he asked in astonishment. 'How do we afford that?'

'Have you never heard of a mortgage,' she asked in a sarcastic tone.

'Of course I have,' he replied rather tetchily. 'How much do we still owe?'

'That's your area, my dear, but I think it's only a few thousand, now,' Julie replied. 'It's all about inflation, isn't it? Our first house was under thirty thousand. That

was a nice little two bed-roomed bungalow in Grimston. When Sarah came along, we moved into a bigger three bed-roomed house nearby. I can't remember the price of that, but we had to take out a bigger mortgage, I know that.'
Rob remembered when a house near his parents' went on the market for just under ten thousand pounds. That was in 1978 and his parents were amazed at that. They had only paid three hundred and fifty pounds for theirs when they first got married. How times had changed.
Rob and Julie were now skirting an area of marshy ground to their right and heading for a lone building near a rickety jetty beside a creek.
'This is all very pretty,' Rob said, looking through the viewfinder of his camera to try to frame the scene as best he could. A Land Rover parked next to the building was ruining the best angle looking down the creek. He tried crouching down to achieve an artistic angle but his knees and back were so much stiffer than he expected and abandoned the idea. It was too muddy to consider kneeling or lying down. He wandered around to the other side of the building but then the light was wrong.
'Last year, you took a very nice telephoto shot from the higher bank,' Julie said, pointing to the opposite side of the road where a few cars had been parked. He followed her suggestion and climbed the path to the bank but the Land Rover still spoiled the image so he abandoned the idea. He was still in the mindset of not wanting to waste film even though he now knew he could delete unsuccessful images from his camera.
'It's called the Coal Barn,' Julie said, pointing at the building. 'We don't know why. Perhaps they used to unload coal there ... or perhaps they just stored it for use with the fishing boats. I keep meaning to look it up on the internet, but I always forget.'

They now turned their attention seawards where numerous small birds were feeding on the muddy banks of the many creeks and old timbers rose eerily from the glutinous mud. 'What are those birds?' Rob asked.
'You told me last, year,' she replied. 'I think the ones with the long probing beaks are oystercatchers. I know one of the others is some kind of plover – and, of course, there are some gulls ... but look,' she added in an excited voice, 'there is an egret like I told you.'
'That's definitely not a baby eagle,' Rob said. 'There's another over there.' He looked through his viewfinder but even with the longest telephoto setting, the image was too small to capture.
'We'd better get going,' Julie said. 'We've still got a way to go.'
Rob took a few pictures looking out towards the sea across a creek and used the old timbers as foreground. He really wanted to linger. He was in his home county. He knew nothing about Rutland except what he had learned in the last ten days. Norfolk was where his heart lay, as much as he had liked what little he had seen of his new county. But the coast path along the bank looked inviting so he replaced his lens cap and proceeded with their walk, all the time gazing around at the big skies and the distant views over the flat landscape. He dearly wished he did remember the area because it was wonderful and he wished that he had shared it with Kate. Perhaps he had, but somehow, he felt not.
As they walked along, his mind went back to an earlier conversation. 'How much do we still owe on our mortgage?' he asked.
'Now you're asking. You'd have been able to tell me a couple of weeks ago before your accident. Let's think ... I think we're paying about four hundred a month ... and

we've got three more years to go, so you can work that out.
'Just over fourteen thousand,' he replied quite quickly just to prove his brain was still working even if his memory wasn't. 'That sounds like a lot of money.'
'It's not as much as Ben and Sarah have to pay,' Julie responded.
'Building Societies usually let you borrow two and half times your salary,' Rob said. He had investigated that while making plans to propose to Kate.
'You're a bit out of touch, my love,' she said. 'No one would ever be able to buy a house if that was still the case. You couldn't buy a small terraced house for that amount. On our earnings, which aren't that bad, we'd have to find a place for ...' she hesitated. She was good at arithmetic but not as quick as Rob '... a hundred and fifty thousand. You might get a beach hut for that.'
'So we're earning about sixty thousand a year between us,' he said, again demonstrating his powers of mental arithmetic. He assumed that he being the man, he would be earning the bigger part of that and it made him feel good.
'Yeah, I think that's about right,' she replied not mentioning that she contributed almost two thirds of their earnings.
'Is that a good amount by today's standards?' he asked still trying to get to grips with the value of money in 2019.
'I think that's quite good,' she replied with a nod. 'We haven't always been so comfortable. I stopped work when we had children and that was a tough period for us. We had to forego a lot of luxuries and didn't have a proper holiday for several years, but I used the time while stuck at home to study with the Open University and got my degree in Business Studies. I'm a BA, you know.'

Now it occurred to him that maybe he wasn't the main breadwinner. Perhaps they were more equal than he had first thought.
'Well done, you,' he said and looked at her with even more admiration.
'I couldn't have done it without your support, you know. You gave me lots of help and did more than your fair share of housework and minding the children. But it paid off. I got my next job because my new boss had been impressed. He said getting my degree while raising a family showed that I had a good work ethic.'
'I'm sure you have,' he said, as they approached the RSPB hides outside Holme-next-the-sea.
'Is any of this ringing a bell?' she asked sweeping her arms around the scenery.
'I'm afraid not,' he replied, 'but I am enjoying it – apart from my aching knees. Do I suffer from arthritis?'
'Yes, a little. Have you been taking your glucosamine regularly?'
'When I remember,' he said. 'I may have missed a few days.'
'You must remember,' she said firmly. 'This is probably the result of you playing football all those years. You didn't retire until you were forty. I think there's a bench coming up soon. We can stop to rest your knees and have a drink.'
'So I haven't played for twenty years,' he said, wistfully. 'Mind you, I don't think I could last five minutes, now.'
'You used to take Ben to the junior teams when he was younger. I think you enjoyed that nearly as much as playing yourself, although you did used to get a bit uptight at times. There's the bench,' she said, pointing ahead.
Rob was much relieved to sit down. 'How much further?' he asked.

‘I think we’re over halfway,’ Julie said. ‘Last year, we walked all the way to Hunstanton, but we had a bit more time that day ... and we stopped for lunch at the cafe, but it always gets busy, so we’ll press on when we’ve rested a little.’

The last few hundred yards of their walk through Holme was over tarmac and both of them were flagging in the heat of midday, but Julie urged them on as they had to catch their bus or they would be waiting around for a further half hour. As it was, they only had to wait five minutes.

As they boarded the bus behind another couple, Julie saw the other people paying with a contactless card and urged Rob to do the same, which was better than offering a ten pound note and receiving an admonishment from the driver. This was all a new experience for Rob who had expected to see a conductor collecting the fares.

Once seated, he wanted to ask Julie how a contactless payment worked, but the bus was busy and his conversation might have been overheard. He decided that he didn’t want to look a complete idiot in front of everyone.

‘We need to look out for our stop and press the bell or the driver may not stop,’ Julie said, pointing to the bell across the aisle.

‘You’d better tell me when,’ he replied. The driver seemed to be in a hurry and they were soon dismounting opposite the cafe.

‘They look a little busy,’ Julie said, ‘but there is one table free, so I think we’ve got time for a cup of tea. I want to use their facilities before we set off for Ben’s. Now that you know how to use your card for a contactless payment, you can buy us a pot of tea.’

Chapter 18

In 1979, Rob's idea of a day on the coast would have entailed a wander around Wells-Next-The-Sea or Hunstanton, either of which would have probably included a bag of fish and chips or an ice cream. He had no knowledge of the coast path and would have considered a walk between two small villages as a waste of time as long as he had access to a car or even a bus service. Nevertheless, he had enjoyed this walk despite the complaints from his knees. A pot of tea had restored his energy levels and he was now ready to drive back to his old haunts around King's Lynn, although he wasn't sure about meeting his new family of strangers.

As they set off towards North Wootton, Rob had a strange feeling that he wasn't going to enjoy this particular journey. Julie sensed his nervousness. 'Are you all right, Rob?' she asked.

He sighed. He didn't really know how to answer and just replied 'Yeah ... it's been a bit of a long day.' That wasn't strictly true as it was barely the middle of the afternoon, but he didn't know how else to explain his feelings.

He would have liked to have left the main coast road to visit Hunstanton, but Julie insisted that they headed straight to Ben's. 'We don't want to be too late getting home, so we want to allow enough time to spend with them,' she said.

The holiday traffic was starting to build up and the roundabout at the southern end of Hunstanton confused him, with much of the traffic coming from a new road from his right, meaning he had to give way and be patient until a suitable gap appeared.

A further roundabout to the north of Snettisham also confused him until Julie directed him onto the bypass, which hadn't existed in 1979. The traffic was now even slower and his feelings of unease had not lessened.
At the end of the bypass, he was then on more familiar territory which should have relaxed him but it didn't.
As they left Babingley and headed up the hill, Julie said 'You know we turn off along here where it's signposted to Castle Rising.'
'Yes, of course,' he replied, but as he pulled into the central reservation, he started to panic. Cars were hurtling towards him down the hill and he started to shake. His hands gripped the steering wheel so tightly that Julie thought his knuckles were going to break through the skin.
'I can't do it,' he said, almost crying. 'I can't do it!'
'Rob? Whatever is the problem?' Julie asked reaching out to hold his left hand which was clamped to the steering wheel.
'I can't move,' he said.
'Of course you can,' she said. 'Just put it in gear and wait for a gap in the traffic.'
But gaps came and went and still Rob gripped the wheel and wouldn't budge. The driver behind sounded his horn.
'Come on, love. Someone behind is waiting for you to move.'
Another car joined the queue behind them. The central reservation was not very big and if anyone else joined the queue, it would be very dangerous, but still Rob sat transfixed.
Julie looked behind at the driver who was sounding his horn a second time and saw two other cars signalling to join their queue. 'We must move or there's going to be a nasty accident,' she said. 'Look, after this red car, there's a very big gap. Put it into gear and get ready.'

Rob did as she instructed and started revving the engine like a nervous learner driver waiting to release the clutch. The red car passed and he shot over the road, but ground to a halt barely twenty yards into the new road. The impatient driver gave another blast as he overtook Rob's stationary vehicle. Julie gave him a one-fingered salute which was as much as a release valve as it was bad-tempered reaction. She turned on the hazard warning lights while Rob slumped over the steering wheel.

'I killed her,' he sobbed.

'What?'

'I killed her.'

'Who?

'Kate ... I killed her.' He was now sobbing.

'We can't talk about this here,' Julie said. 'We're causing a bit of an obstruction. Let's drive to the *Black Horse* and park there.'

He took out a handkerchief and dried his eyes. He looked at her. 'I'm all right now. I'm back,' but she could see that he was still upset.

As he drove off, he reached his hand out to squeeze Julie's knee. Now she knew that he was back. She patted the back of his hand and said 'That's better,' and realising that the hazard lights were still flashing, she turned them off.

He let out a big sigh and said 'You all right, mate? That must have scared you.'

'I'm all right, mate,' she said, knowing that only her true husband would call her *mate.*

He parked in the far corner of the pub car park, next to the ancient church. He turned off the engine and opened the two front windows. Everything was quiet. They knew that the pub had been closed for a few years but had also heard that it was under new management and was now either open again or soon to be so.

'We'd been out for an evening meal,' Rob said. 'I'm not sure where. It was a long while ago. It might have been *The Gin Trap* at Ringstead. I asked her if she would like to get engaged. She agreed and we were both feeling ecstatic as we drove home along that same stretch of road. We'd shared a bottle of wine, although I was just under the limit. They tested me, apparently. It was September so it was dark. I got to that same junction ready to turn off. I was in a bit of a hurry 'cause I needed a pee. There was a gap coming up and I knew I could make it even though the other car was coming down the hill quite fast although it's not always easy to judge speed in the dark. But as I pulled across, the car stuttered. It was due a service and I'd been putting it off. I'd been having a few problems with the timing, but that wasn't a job that I could tackle. Cars didn't have fuel injection in those days – well, not mine anyway.

'I heard the other car braking and I think he swerved a little to the inside but he still caught us a glancing blow. He hit the side where Kate was sitting.' Rob paused to sniff back his emotion.

'It was a Sunday night and the road wasn't that busy so it was a while apparently before the ambulance arrived. All of this, I found out later. There were no mobile phones then so I don't know how they summoned the ambulance. I woke up in hospital two days later with a few bad scratches and bruises. I must have had a similar blow to the head like I did two weeks ago. When I heard what had happened and that Kate was dead, I was naturally inconsolable. It was my fault. I'd had too much to drink – not over the limit, mind, but still too much – and I should have had the car serviced. It was a while before I could get in a car again. It was such a traumatic experience that I must have blanked it all out

of my memory because I soon realised that I couldn't remember the incident – until now, of course.'
Julie hadn't spoken during his tale, but now she said 'Didn't one of the doctors say they thought your memory loss could be due to some kind of trauma? It all makes sense now, doesn't it?'
'Yes, I suppose it does. If we saw this in a TV drama, we'd say what a load of old nonsense. I'm so sorry to have put you though all this. It hasn't been much fun, has it?'
'No, my love,' she said with a huge grin. 'But you're back now. I'm going to keep you away from trees and rockeries. Now we'd better get around Ben's and tell them the good news.'
Rob let out a sigh. 'I hope Tamsin hasn't made one of her fruit cakes. If she has, I'm going to tell her I don't like them.'
'No, you won't,' replied Julie realising that this was certainly proof that her Rob was back. 'You'll tell her you just want a small piece and wash it down with a cup of tea. She is quite a good cook really; it's just her baking that lets her down.'

'Grandad!' said young George, as Rob was the first to enter his son's house. He was closely followed by Julie. 'Nanny!' and George ran to greet his grandmother.
'I can see my place in his affections,' said Rob. 'Hello George. Don't I get a hug?'
'In a minute,' replied George. 'I'm busy hugging Nanny.'
They all laughed at his precociousness.
'Grandad wants a hug,' said Julie. 'He's been a little poorly, but he's all right now.'
Ben and Tamsin both expressed their pleasure at the news. 'How did that happen? Did you get another bang on the head?' asked Ben.

‘Not quite ... just a bit of shock treatment.’ He thought it best not to bring up tales about an old girlfriend. ‘Any chance of a cup of tea ‘round here? Your mother’s been dragging me out on one her little walks again and I’m dehydrated.’
‘I’ll put the kettle on,’ said Tamsin. ‘I’ve made a cake.’
‘Just a small piece for me, please,’ said Rob. ‘I have to watch my sugar levels.’ That was a lie but it sounded genuine.
‘It’s banoffee pie,’ said Ben and Rob was already having second thoughts. ‘I expect you’ve had an interesting couple of weeks,’ he added.
‘Yes,’ said Rob. ‘It’s amazing how life has moved on since 1979 – like that wonderful thing you have in your car that is always giving you instructions as you drive along.’
‘You mean the Satnav?’ Ben said.
‘No, I mean a wife,’ Rob replied and he heard Tamsin’s lovely little giggle from the kitchen.
‘At least, if it was a Satnav,’ said Ben, ‘you can turn it off.’
‘I heard that,’ said Tamsin still in the kitchen.
Rob liked Tamsin. He hadn’t when he first met her. He had considered her to be a silly little giggling dimwit not good enough for his son, but with hindsight, it was just her nervousness at meeting Ben’s parents for the first time. In any case, she had still been quite young at that time. Now, Rob found her funny little giggle to be quite endearing and only employed when she found something to be amusing rather than a nervous reaction. She was a slender little thing with engaging dark eyes and looked so delicate when standing next to her strapping husband who was taller than Rob by three inches. Today, Ben was sporting the start of yet another beard to replace the one he shaved off to attend a friend’s wedding. Rob had never bothered with

facial hair. He found anything more than a one day growth to be irritating and Julie seemed to agree with him, yet liked to see Ben's growth.
The banoffee pie was delicious and Rob was pleased to accept a second offering despite his earlier warning about his sugar levels.
The conversation within the group revolved around young George and Rob found himself drifting off into his own thoughts about Kate. He hadn't thought much about her for nearly forty years but his recent bang on the head had brought it all back. There was no regret in his decision to marry Julie, but he still wondered what would have happened if he hadn't had that extra glass of wine in 1979.
As he mulled this all over in his head, he was suddenly aware that the family were all looking at him. 'We're talking to you, Rob,' his wife said.
'I'm sorry,' he said. 'Where am I? Is this Ben's family?'
The room went quiet. He looked around the room and returned their stares one by one. 'Just kidding!' he said.

Epilogue

Rob and Jed sat outside *The White Horse,* drinking their beer. This is what they usually did after a morning's canoeing on Rutland Water. It was their first time since Rob's accident and he was pleased to be back in the swing of things. Because he would be working later in the day, Rob had only ordered a half pint whereas Jed, with no such responsibilities, was eagerly consuming a full pint. His motto was 'soldiers don't drink halves.'

'Did your memory come back gradually?' Jed asked.

'No, I had a flashback to an accident in 1979 and suddenly, I could remember everything.'

'How strange! You must have felt really great about that?' Jed asked.

'Of course. I was beginning to wonder if it would ever happen. Julie was the same, but it's funny, you know ... I know it was a bad experience, but at the same time, I was learning new things every day ... and that was nice. As it was with my relationship with Julie. It was like dating a new girl. I was getting more and more fond of her ... and I think I was falling in love with her all over again. It gave me a very warm feeling. And, of course, in 1979, my sex life was a bit patchy; and now I could have it more or less whenever I wanted – or rather whenever we wanted, which isn't always the same.'

Jed laughed. 'What have you learned from your experience?' he asked.

'That's the kind of question we were all asked at the end of that dreadful Team Building course you organised,' Rob replied. "*What have we all learned from this course*?" asked that annoying trainer. "*Bugger all*" is what nearly everyone called out.'

'Yeah, well, if it's any consolation, I didn't enjoy it either,' said Jed. 'I was told that I had to organise something like that or I would have lost my training budget. It was a call centre, not the SAS planning a dangerous rescue mission. In fact, it did more harm than good. Sam came out of the course thinking he was destined to be a Team Leader. He left four months later when I told him that it wasn't going to happen.'

'Good riddance is what I say,' said Rob. 'He was always a pain in the arse.'

'At least it was a nice hotel,' said Jed. 'Anyway, you haven't answered my question.'

'No, you mean my little sabbatical, don't you? That's what I call those two weeks now. I can't think of a better way of referring to it. Well, I learned an awful lot. It was amazing how much had changed in the world in those missing forty years – some for the good; other things not so good.'

'Like what?' Jed asked.

'Well, for one thing, cars are so much better these days - fuel injection; power steering; better brakes; better stereo, and so on, but the roads are busier – and they're in worse condition than they were. Working conditions are better and there are far more women working full-time. When we had our children, it was quite normal for wives to stop working to bring them up. I don't think I'd ever heard of a child-minder in those days, although richer people might have had a nanny or taken on an au pair. Going to university was the exception, not the rule. Firms offering apprenticeships were a much better alternative. I was a trainee surveyor with a couple of A levels. Nowadays, I would need a degree to get such a job.

'And then, of course, there are all the fancy gadgets you get these days. I couldn't believe it when I saw Julie talking to our son face to face on the 'phone – just like *Star Trek.* When I had that accident in 1979, a mobile 'phone may well have saved Kate's life. I don't know that, of course, but it's just a thought. Mind you, for so many people, mobile 'phones have taken over their lives. When I went into Stamford one morning, all I could see were people wandering down the street staring at their devices like a hoard of zombies.

'And don't get me started on the television programmes. When I saw all those channels and the hundreds of programmes, I thought everyone in Britain must be glued to their sets twenty four hours a day, but after a few days, I realised that nearly everything was a repeat – and those things that weren't were rubbish. I was all right because I hadn't seen any of the repeats before but Julie was getting fed up with me watching all the things she already seen several times.'

'I'm sure she was very patient with you,' said Jed. 'What about people and their attitudes? How do you think they have changed since 1979?'

Rob had a notion what Jed was aiming at. He thought carefully before answering, taking a long swig of his beer. 'Well ... two weeks ago, during my sabbatical, I doubt if I would have been sitting here with you if I had know then what I know now about you. It wasn't that I had anything against gay people ...' He hesitated, determined to get the right words. '... It was more a thing at that time that if you were friendly with gay people, someone might automatically assume that you, too, were gay – and I would have been mortified if anyone thought that about me. I probably still would, but I think people are less inclined these days to make that assumption.

'You have to remember, that even although more people were *coming out* in the seventies, there were still a lot of people who weren't. If you lived in Los Angeles, or New York, or even London, there was a lot more ... shall we say ... celebration of being gay ... but in little old King's Lynn where I was living in 1979, there

was very little ... um, action in that respect.'
Rob looked across at his friend to see if he had offended him.
'It's all right, Rob. I know exactly what you're saying.'
Rob felt a little relieved. 'Were you open about it at that time?' he asked.
'I'd just joined the army,' said Jed. 'I couldn't afford to be open about it then.'
'No, I suppose not,' said Rob.
'In any case, I didn't really want to come out until after I left the army. I'd had a few girlfriends before then. None of them really worked out and I never came close to marrying. Girls like a soldier, but don't necessarily want the life that goes with it. As things turned out, that was probably for the best. Anyway, how's work?'
Rob was pleased that Jed had changed the subject. He had found the previous topic a little uncomfortable. 'It's great,' he replied. 'It's good to get back in the old routine.'
'How's Mrs Pumphrey?' Jed asked. He was referring to the lady whose husband had splashed out on a home gym. The reference to Mrs Pumphrey was because of the character in *All Creatures Great and Small* by James Herriot who would never stick to the diet imposed upon her little Tricky Woo.
'Still ignoring everything I tell her,' said Rob. 'She's fine when I go around. She gets stuck into the exercises that I give her and she says all the right things, but I know as soon as I leave, she'll be making arrangements to see her friends, eating and drinking all the wrong things. She says she has to entertain lots of people because of her husband's business, which I'm sure is true but I feel that she's wasting her money with me.'
'Why should you care?' said Jed. 'If she ever achieved her goals in terms of her weight and her fitness, she

might not need you anymore.'
'It's a case of professional pride,' said Rob. 'I see her as a challenge. If I succeed with her, and she told some of her friends, I might get some extra business. Like the Mrs Pumphrey in the book, she showers me with gifts which I feel guilty about. It's a good thing that Julie is not the jealous type or she might wonder why I keep coming home with bottles of champagne and expensive aftershave.'
'Perhaps I should become a personal trainer,' said Jed. 'I did enough fitness training in the army – and I wouldn't object to the odd bottle of champagne.'
'I thought you enjoyed being retired,' said Rob, knowing that his friend was only kidding.
'Another thing,' Rob continued, 'it was kind of funny, going from being a fit twenty year old, playing all sorts of sports, to suddenly being a sixty year old with aches and pains in places that I didn't know you could have aches and pains. And having to take medication every day.
'Did I ever tell you about the time I went for a check up? This pretty little nurse was doing my blood tests and so on. She was lovely. I asked her if she thought it was all right for me to still be masturbating at my age.
'She said "Will you keep still. I'm trying to take your blood pressure."'
Jed laughed. 'For a moment, I thought you really did ask her that question. There was no pretty nurse, was there?'
'I think I heard Jethro telling that one,' Rob said. 'He's funny.
'Anyway, there is one other thing that I've learnt from my little sabbatical. I think I've learned to appreciate things a lot more. Julie and I have not always had things easy. It was tough for a few years when I was made redundant and then had to get a job in a call

centre, doing all that travelling for a job that offered little reward – no offence, Jed, but it didn't. Because of that, I was seldom able to spend time with my children when they were still growing up and it's only in the last few years that things have come good.

'The last few weeks have made me realise that I have a wonderful wife, a wonderful family and a nice home. Of course, I feel bad about losing Kate, but if she hadn't died in 1979, I would never have married Julie, so you could say that because of a bang on the head, I'm going to appreciate what I have so much more.'

Mark's Out of Eleven

By

Will Stebbings

Published by Troubador Publishing Ltd

It's September 1960. Mark Barker has passed his eleven-plus and has followed his brother into Parkside Grammar School for boys. Having two sons at a Grammar School places a huge burden on his working class family and he is already wearing his brother's hand-me-down blazer, while all around him are wearing brand new uniforms.

The Headmaster at Parkside likes to run the school with an iron discipline and frequently punishes miscreants with the cane, putting a tremendous fear into this sensitive young boy. The pupils also fear Mr Tucker, the evil Sports Master who is not aversed to physical violence to instil discipline.

Having been split from his old primary school friends, Mark now seeks to forge new friendships and is reasonably successful, but he is unable to shake off the annoying Jarvis who is forever trying to crack silly jokes. He gets Mark into bother with his strict Form Master when he passes him pictures of nude ladies. Mark also receives his first detention when Jarvis snitches on him.

At first, Mark is pleased that there are no girls at his school, but when puberty strikes, he finds himself discovering new sensations. His encounters with girls are few and far between, but when they occur, it leaves him perturbed and frustrated. However, if encounters with the opposite sex cause him anguish, those with the same sex confuse him even further. His new softly-spoken friend Lenny talks in sexual innuendos and when Mark discovers the truth about Lenny and his friend Toots, he has to tackle his prejudices head on.

ISBN : 9781788037891

Off the Mark

By

Will Stebbings

Published by Troubador Publishing Ltd

This story charts the progress of Mark Barker, who leaves an all boys' Grammar School in 1965, having absolutely no experience of girls or, indeed, the world as a whole.

The scene is set in the first chapter by his amusing recollections of the time he spent at school where the staff were a curious mixture of sadists and perverts. We also get an insight into life in the sixties for a working class family in a small Norfolk town.

Mark's first day in his first job is fraught with uncomfortable experiences. Every mistake is taken to heart, but he is a quick learner and soon establishes himself. The story reminds us of life before computers, calculators and modern photocopiers. Mark had a reputation at school as being a bit of a joker and he seeks to establish a similar reputation at work, so the story is littered with comical incidents.

He loves 60's soul music and enjoys playing football. He is also a very shy youth who lacks confidence in his ability to attract girls and ends up forming attractions to all the wrong girls for all the wrong reasons.

His unusual encounter with the mini-skirted Blodwyn forces him to question his own sexuality and desires.

He meets the lovely Pauline, whom he considers to be the most beautiful girl he has ever met, yet he falls for the plain and waspish Karen, who breaks his heart by her total lack of compassion.

He tries to look beyond Karen to find a girlfriend, but every time he gets close to getting a date, something goes wrong and his thoughts return to Karen. Unsuccessful blind dates and foursomes only serve to exacerbate the loneliness of this sensitive teenager, as he scrapes through to manhood and attempts to get 'off the mark.'

ISBN : 9781780881522

Further Off the Mark

By

Will Stebbings

Published by Troubador Publishing Ltd

This story is the amusing successor to *Off the Mark.* In this latest book, nineteen year-old Mark Barker is moving on from his youthful awkwardness, but he is still seeking to expand on his paltry experience of girls of the opposite sex. He pursues and sometimes dates a variety of young women, including the lovely Sandy who shares his love of Soul Music; as does her equally attractive and flirtatious mother, causing Mark much anguish and confusion, but as with most of his encounters, he often confuses love with lust!
As he tries to establish a new career, Marks makes enemies; wrecking his chances of advancement, but there is a consolation in his new attractive female assistant – and, of course, Mark develops an infatuation for her!
The novel is set in Norfolk in the late sixties and is a nostalgic journey to a simpler time when a 'discotheque evening' was a new concept and when unreliable cars could be coaxed into action by jumping up and down on their door sills!

ISBN : 9781783062102

Completely Off the Mark

By

Will Stebbings

Published by 3P Publishing Ltd

It is 1971. Mark Barker has a steady girlfriend and a promising career as a Computer Programmer. To make his life complete, he now owns the car that he has always coveted – a Wolseley 1500. Life couldn't get any better.

Except that his girlfriend has to go away to look after a sick parent. Mark could visit her eighty miles away but his treasured vehicle has failed its MOT and has succumbed to the dreaded rust bug. In fact, it is rusting away before his eyes. To make matters worse, after just two years as a programmer, he has completed all the programming work and there is little left to justify his continued employment.

So he is now without a girlfriend, without transport and planning for yet another career change. At first, he is typically despondent at his bad luck, but he is determined to turn his life around.

A colleague tells him that young Polly would like to go out with him, but he is unimpressed by her thin emaciated appearance. By the time that she has her anorexia under control and has blossomed into a voluptuous beauty, there is too much competition from younger studs and he fails in his quest to date her.

He encounters two attractive ladies at an evening class. He and Claire hit it off, but he burns his bridges with her by pursuing the other lady, Margaret, whose lifestyle revolves around horses and sports cars and he is soon made to realise that he isn't able to live up to her extravagant expectations.
Then he encounters Helen and a new challenge presents itself.
In this latest novel about Mark Barker, Will Stebbings provides another humorous and nostalgic page turner for his loyal readers. Set in West Norfolk, *Completely Off the Mark* is another easy to read story, filled with nostalgia for the time, with tales of lust and romance.

ISBN : 9781911559993

Tess of the Dormobiles

By

Will Stebbings

Published by KDP

Theresa Finbow is an author who has taken a cottage in a quiet area of Norfolk while she starts work on her next novel which is to be called *Tess of the Dormobiles*. Tess, the central character in this new book, is someone who craves adventure, so Theresa seeks to emulate her in order to gain inspiration for her work, but this brings her into contact with Billy, a local farm worker who has a malevolent stare and is reputed to have a violent temper. He has also been implicated in the death of his ex-girlfriend. So after a terrifying incident with Billy, Theresa invites her estranged husband to come to her rescue, but after a short visit, Danny returns home, leaving Theresa to face her demons alone, one of whom is Billy's elder brother who is capable of inflicting even greater horrors on Theresa.

ISBN : 9781515235057

Printed in Great Britain
by Amazon